MY EX'S DAD

AN AGE GAP, MOUNTAIN MAN ROMANCE

K.C. CROWNE

Copyright © 2023 by K.C. Crowne

All rights reserved.

No part of this book may be reproduced in any form or by any electronic or mechanical means, including information storage and retrieval systems, without written permission from the author, except for the use of brief quotations in a book review.

 Created with Vellum

DESCRIPTION

"*Meet my Dad, Jack.*"
A lump forms in my throat as I hold back panic.
I'm standing face to face with my mystery one night stand.
I just learned the handsome silver fox mountain man is my ex's dad.
And the person planning his son's wedding? Yours truly!

Months ago, a sexy silver-fox saved my life.
All I knew was a hot, bearded mountain man showed up right when I needed it.

He asked me to spend the rest of the night with him in his mountain cabin - and I thanked him with great pleasure.

It was the most erotic night of my life.
But I never thought I'd see the mystery mountain man again - until he comes back into my life in the most unexpected way imaginable!

In public, we pretend there's nothing between us.
Yet, behind closed doors, we can't keep our clothes on.

And to add fuel to this inferno of a fire…
I've been keeping a secret that could change everything.

How do you tell a man with a dangerous lifestyle, set against having more children, that he'll be a father again?

Readers note: This is full-length standalone, ex's dad, older man, surprise pregnancy romance. You'll need a cool glass of water because the HEAT level is scorching. K.C. Crowne is an Amazon Top 8 Bestseller and International Bestselling Author.

CHAPTER 1

BETH

"Whoa, easy!"
A flash of horse tail accompanied by a piercing whinny nearly knocked me off my damn feet. Margo, my Palomino, did *not* want to go outside. I hurriedly placed my hand on her ivory white mane, stroking her slowly in an effort to calm her down.

"There we are, sweetie," I said, speaking softly. "That's it."

Margo, good girl that she was, calmed down right away. It was unlike her to get worked up like that. Out of the three horses we had on the family farm, she was easily the most mellow and easy to handle. When I caught sight of the pasture through the open barn door and spotted flurries of snow dancing on the early winter wind, I realized right away what was wrong.

"I swear, girl," I said, a smile on my face. "You've always been afraid of the snow—ever since you were a dang foal."

Margo snorted, her big, dark eyes situated on the open door, as if on guard. With her white mane, golden coat and powerful muscles, Margo was about as gorgeous as horses came.

"Well, let me tell you about a concept I learned back in college. It's called exposure therapy. You ever heard of that?"

Margo kept her eyes on the snow as I hopped up on a nearby worktable, clapping my hands onto my knees.

"It means that if you're afraid of something, like spiders or the dark, or in your case my fine-coated friend, a little snow, the best way to get over it is to expose yourself to it a little at a time."

Another snort, timed perfectly to appear as if she were dismissing the concept altogether.

"Now, now," I said, holding up my gloved hands. "I know it sounds a little crazy on the surface. But trust me—I think it could do you wonders."

I hopped off the workstation and headed over to the barn door. I looked out to the huge stretch of pasture of our Colorado farm, the Rockies rising in the distance. The grass was dusted with snow, the air chilly enough to make me pull my shearling coat a little tighter.

"See? Nothing to be worried about. Just a little fresh winter powder to invigorate."

I couldn't speak for Margo, but I was eager as hell to get out there. I'd spent the last few hours holed up in my room going over legal documents, trying to make heads or tails of the convoluted legalese within. Some fresh air sounded like just the thing to get my mind right.

Margo, on the other hand, didn't want to budge. I turned, putting my hands on my hips.

"Alright, girl. Lucky for you, I'm not above a little bribery now and then. So, how about this; we go out there for a little while and when we get back, I might let you have a few of those apple-oatmeal treats you can't get enough of."

Margo let out another snort and stamped her hoof. She was responding to my gentle tone more than anything, but sometimes talking to her felt like negotiating with a misbehaving toddler—a massive, furry toddler.

I stroked her mane a few more times, making certain that she was calm and ready to be taken out. When I was confident Margo was good to go, I went to work strapping on her riding gear and leading her out of the barn.

Another cold draft hit me as I stepped out, snow curling on the wind. I buttoned my coat the rest of the way, pulling the collar up against the back of my neck.

"Kinda chilly out, huh?" I asked Margo. "Well, it'll be good to get out, stretch those legs of yours a bit. Don't want you getting fat on us, right?" I gave her haunches a pat before shutting the barn door.

I turned my attention back to the trail. The sky had darkened in the short amount of time I'd been in the barn, the western distance over the mountains having grown a few shades dimmer. It was enough to give me pause and wonder whether or not it was a good idea to take Margo out after all.

"Don't tell me you're going for a ride, Bee?"

I didn't need to turn to recognize the English-accented voice as my dad's. He approached out of the corner of my eye, leading one of the younger horses back to the barn.

"Why, don't you think I'm up to it?" I flashed Dad a smile.

Dad approached, dressed in his usual outfit of rugged jeans with an equally rugged fur-lined denim jacket, a gray page cap on his head and light brown boots. Dad was tall and strapping, with the same sable hair and light green eyes as mine. Most of my other features, like my lean, dancer's physique, were from Mom.

His face was weathered but handsome. I watched as his eyes narrowed as they often did in an expression of intelligent scanning. Dad was an interesting man, a perfect blend of the English sophistication of his place of birth and the outdoorsy ruggedness of his chosen home in the States.

Dad allowed himself a small smile. "You wouldn't ever catch me saying something so ludicrous, love." He adjusted his hat and turned his attention toward the horizon. "Only that the weather's looking a bit rough. Phone says that we're due for a bit of a snowfall here in a short while—as if those mean-looking clouds aren't all the indication one needs."

"They're still a ways off," I said. "Besides, I wasn't planning on going out for all that long, just a quick trot around Wheeler Hill then back down. Shouldn't take any longer than thirty minutes."

My father regarded me with a bit of skepticism before turning his attention to the clouds once more, as if they might've eased up in the last minute.

"I know better than to try and talk you down once you've set your mind to something, Bee."

I winked. "That's right. And it's what you love about me."

He laughed. "That may be the case. But it's also the trait of yours responsible for these gray hairs I've sprouted over the years."

"That and the fact that you're not getting any younger." I smiled and nudged him with my elbow as I spoke, letting the old man know I was only messing around.

I nodded and smiled at the horse Dad had been leading. "How's the new girl?"

"Oh, Butterscotch here?" he chuckled, giving the

horse a pat. "As sweet as they come. Already have a prospective buyer in mind. As long as her training continues as it has, she should be ready for her new home in a month or so."

Training horses was the bread and butter of business at Wheeler Ranch.

He smiled back, shaking his head. "Well, get on with it. We'll discuss dinner when you're back. I believe your mother was keen on going into town tonight, though I suppose that all depends on what the weather has in store for us."

I tipped my hat before climbing up on Margo and settling in.

"Be back before you know it!" With that, I nudged Margo with my heels, watching as Dad gave me a final wave before leading the horse into the barn.

I glanced downward, holding on to the brim of my hat against another hard gust of wind. Margo kept on straight and steady, but I could feel the nervousness quaking through her.

"You're doing just fine, girl," I said, stroking her side as she moved. "See? That mean old snow isn't so bad."

Margo let out another snort but kept moving forward all the same. The closer I drew to Wheeler Hill, the more I could make out the darkness of the clouds ahead. Part of me wondered if Dad was right, that it'd been a bad idea to go out with this kind of weather on the horizon. I slipped my phone out of my pocket, a picture of Margo on the lock screen. With a few quick swipes, I opened the hourly weather forecast.

It was looking rough. A large snowstorm was set to arrive in the next couple of hours, with a predicted eight to ten inches of snow. All the more reason to make the trek in good time. So long as Margo cooperated, we'd be back within the hour.

I spent the time it took to reach Wheeler's Hill going over my plans for the next few months, specifically those relating to the wedding planning business I'd been putting together, although it wasn't yet much to speak of. I'd spent all of last year learning everything I could about both running a small business and the wedding planning industry. So far, all I'd had to show for it was exactly two clients, one of them a family friend.

I'd set aside a little money that I'd earned from each event, but I hadn't been able to land my next wedding. The ranch occupied a ton of my time, and as much as I loved living with Mom and Dad, it was hard as hell to keep my up-and-coming business separate from life on the ranch.

In short, I needed an office. With an office, I'd finally be able to get my business off the ground. An office would be a place I could go to and focus, to have meetings, to give *Beth's Dream Weddings*—my business name—the feeling of being, well, *a business*. Denver was only a forty-minute drive from the ranch, which meant the commute wouldn't be much at all.

Mom and Dad had offered to pay for the deposit and the first year's rent of the office. They didn't like to make a big show about it in terms of what clothes they wore or cars they drove or anything like that, but my parents had money. Dad had been an investment banker who'd long since sold his firm for a huge payout, and Mom had been an executive project manager back in England.

None of that mattered to me, England was a lifetime ago. So long ago, in fact, that I didn't even have an accent anymore. Besides, I wanted my business to be *my* thing, something I built with my own two hands. Having my parents simply cut me a check to rent an office seemed hollow. Writing my own check, however... I couldn't imagine anything more satisfying.

A cold rush of wind pulled me back into reality. I looked around, realizing that I'd become so lost in my own thoughts that I hadn't even realized I was nearly at the peak of Wheeler Hill. The name "Wheeler Hill" was something of a misnomer. It was tall, a thousand or so feet high, and afforded a sweeping view of the valley where the ranch was located. A well-worn path weaved upward, aspen and pine trees dusted with snow towering overhead.

It was my favorite place to come when I needed some fresh air, or just to clear my head. Not to mention, the view was killer. When I reached the clearing at the top, a smile spread on my face. The Rockies loomed large to the west, white peaks rising and falling across the length of the horizon.

The ranch was to the east, the gorgeous fifty-five-acre stretch of land nestled down in the valley. The property consisted of a handful of buildings; two barns—one for horses, the other for cows—a guest house, a supply shed, and a three-story home built in classic Colorado chalet style with a pointed roof and wood exterior. The interior of the house had been completely remodeled with just about every modern amenity one could want.

Sometimes I wondered why Mom and Dad had made the decision to leave their old lives behind and start fresh in Colorado. All it took for that question to be answered was a trip to the top of Wheeler Hill, to take in the gorgeous panoramic view of the ranch and Rockies, the sky vast and huge and endless up above.

Off to the west, the other side of the valley was covered in a thick blanket of trees, the endless green reaching all the way to the Rockies in the distance. A few plumes of gray smoke rose here and there from the woods, sure signs and a reminder that people lived out there. I imagined burly men in red flannel, axes slung over their shoulders, a metal mug of whiskey and coffee in hand. Tough, independent sorts of guys that you'd never see in downtown Denver.

I smiled, closing my eyes and letting the fresh, mountain air fill my lungs. Only the cold pinprick of snowfall on my face and the shudder of Margo underneath me brought me back into reality.

I patted Margo's side. "Alright, girl, you've done good. Let's get on back home, alright?"

Margo didn't waste a second before turning, pointing us both in the direction of the path leading back down the hill. I pulled the reins, starting her off into a slow trot down. The path was covered in about a half inch or so of snow.

The precipitation picked up on the way down, swirling through the air, the cold making my cheeks burn. The sun had begun to dip lower, the sky behind the clouds aglow with a soft, dull light. Darkness was growing by the second.

Margo picked up her pace, in spite of what I instructed.

"Easy, girl. Easy."

Between the snow and the cold and the dark, she was getting nervous. I needed to get her back to the barn soon.

Her pace seemed to pick up in direct proportion to the increase in snowfall. We headed down the path, my heart beating faster. I slipped my phone out of my pocket and checked the reception. It was spotty as it always was out there, but I had a couple of bars.

Margo let out a whinny while my eyes were on my phone. I looked up just in time to shove my phone back into my pocket and bring my attention to what she was upset about. I gasped, spotting two black figures crossing the path ahead.

"Whoa, girl!"

Margo did as I asked. At first, the two creatures looked like big, shaggy dogs but it didn't take me long to realize they weren't dogs—they were bears. Black bears, to be specific. They weren't an uncommon animal around the area, though it was strange that they'd come right onto the path. Either way, I wasn't too worried. Black bears could look scary, but they were mostly harmless as long as you gave them their distance and didn't spook them.

"Cubs, Margo," I said, a tinge of relief hitting. "Just a couple of baby bears trying to get home, like you and me. Nothing to worry about."

I stroked Margo's mane slowly, feeling her body shake with nervousness. One of the cubs stopped in the middle of the path, glancing up at me. Despite the initial fear, I had to admit the cub was pretty damn cute. The first cub crossed, then the second. I kept Margo still until they were gone.

"Ready, girl?"

I patted Margo on her side once more, giving her the signal to start moving. She did, taking her first steps with a tiny bit of trepidation.

"Come on."

Margo took some more steps forward, quickening her pace to the kind of trot that would bring us home in due time.

Just as we hit the next bend, I turned to my right just in time to watch as a huge, black form appeared in the woods, dark eyes staring back at me.

I'd been so wrapped up in keeping Margo calm that I'd forgotten one of the first rules of bears: Where there's cubs, you can guarantee that mama bear isn't far behind.

She rose up on her back paws, making herself bigger and letting out a deep growl that Margo didn't care for one bit. Margo rose too, a fright-filled whinny sounding.

"Easy, girl. Easy! Just—"

I didn't have a chance to finish before I tumbled backward, slipping off the horse. For several long seconds the world was a swirling blur as I fell. Pain blasted from my head and hip as I landed on both. Another bray from Margo filled the air, and through bleary eyes I sat up just in time to watch as Margo began tearing down the path without me.

I turned slowly to see the big, hulking mama as dark as a chunk of night itself. I stayed still, my heart beating hard as hell in my chest. Every instinct in my body told me to get up and run for it, but I knew enough to understand that running was the worst move to make when a bear was sizing you up.

Finally, after several moments that stretched out into their own mini eternities, the mama let out a snort as she returned to all fours and began across the path in the direction her cubs had gone. She tossed one more glance in my direction, as if confirming once more that I wasn't a threat, before shuffling off into the woods.

I was alone. The danger having passed, the pain occupied my mind in full force. I'd crashed hard onto my hip, the momentum bouncing my head off the ground. Margo was long gone. Knowing her, she'd bolted straight home to the ranch. If she hadn't, however, my parents wouldn't be happy if I came home without her.

Speaking of home, I needed to get moving. The pain was intense, and as I pushed myself up to standing, a dizziness overcame me that made it hard to stay that way. I staggered to the nearest tree and leaned against it. The dizziness lingered, and the longer I stood, the more I realized I was going to need to call my dad and have him come and get me.

My hand shot to my hip pocket, and I pulled out my phone and quickly brought it to my face. My heart sank down to the soles of my boots as I looked upon the totally smashed screen. When I'd fallen, I'd landed with all my weight on the phone, crushing it to the point of uselessness. I tried in vain to turn the screen back on, but it remained black.

I felt weak. The phone fell from my hand and onto the snowy ground. I stepped back against the tree and slumped down into a sitting position. An incredible fatigue came over me like a heavy blanket, my eyelids drooping more and more...

I needed to get home, and I needed to do it before nightfall and the snowstorm were in full force.

First, I just needed to close my eyes...

CHAPTER 2

JACK

So much for a quiet walk in the woods.

Last thing I wanted to deal with was a pissed-off mama bear.

Buddy, my Australian Shepherd/Border Collie mix, stood at my side, his perked-up ears letting me know he was on high alert, his multicolored coat dusted with fresh snow.

"Stay right there, big guy," I said as I crouched down, holding my palm out a bit in front of me. "Leave it."

Well-trained dog that he was, Buddy stayed right at my side. My other hand hovered near the Magnum revolver I kept at my back hip for the possibility of such an occasion. During my years living in the woods, I'd only ever needed it for the rare warning shot. Truth be told, the idea of having to shoot a bear didn't sit right with me in the slightest. A man needed to be prepared all the same.

The woods ahead shifted, branches moving. Slowly, I lifted my binoculars to my eyes. It was getting dark, and between the setting sun and the snow-filled clouds above, spotting anything in the woods wasn't easy—especially a black bear and her cubs.

I groaned as I stood up.

You're approaching the wrong side of forty, dumbass. About time you started realizing you're not twenty-five anymore.

I chuckled, shaking my head at my internal monologue. I'd been told on more than a few occasions that I could be the cocky sort. To that end, I'd cultivated a mental discussion designed to keep my ass in check. It was true that I was a few years shy of fifty. Maybe it was time I started acting like it.

Maybe. For the time being, I was having too much damn fun.

I held position for a bit longer, making sure that the bears had moved on. As I stood, I glanced up into the trees above. A few different types of birds were there and I passed the time by naming them off.

I let my eyes linger on a Goldfinch for a while, the beautiful golden color of its wings a striking contrast to the greens and whites around it. The bird hopped along the branch before finally taking off, flying into the distance.

Buddy turned his head toward me, letting his tongue hang out as he panted. I reached down and scratched the top of his head.

"Alright. You ready to get a mo—"

Before I could finish my sentence, another rustling sounded out, this time behind me. I turned in the direction of the path up Wheeler Hill—the border of Wheeler Ranch—and watched the trees. I'd expected to see the bear coming back.

It didn't. What *did* race down the path was a horse. The beast was running too damn quickly to get a good look at it, but I could tell by the golden coat that it was likely a Palomino. And the fact that it was loaded up with riding gear told me that it was a tamed and owned horse, not one of those wild mustangs I'd seen around before.

The sight brought questions to mind. Namely—what the hell had happened to the rider?

It looked like the horse was headed in the direction of Wheeler Ranch, a good few miles away. Best guess if I wanted to find who'd been on top of that beast was to head the opposite way. I looked up at the darkening clouds and the storm on the horizon.

"Let's go, Bud," I said, following my words with a sharp whistle. "Let's get moving, see what we can find."

I'd already been out for a few hours. My legs were aching in that good sort of way, the kind where you knew the relief would be instant the moment you plopped your butt down. I'd been looking forward to getting back to the cabin—putting on a fire and spending the rest of the night reading—with some whiskey close at hand while the snow came down outside, Buddy curled up on the rug in front of the fireplace. Nights like those were about as close to heaven as I could imagine.

Eager as I was to get to it, there wasn't a chance I'd be heading home without checking the trail to make sure no one was there. With what I'd seen of the horse, the odds were good I'd find some poor SOB lying hurt and cold.

Buddy and I made our way through the woods in the direction of the trail and it didn't take long before we were on the path and heading up. The snow came down harder, the intensity greater than I'd expected. I pulled my coat tight, glancing down to make sure Buddy was close as we continued up the trail. Good boy that he was, Buddy remained right at my side.

The snow had accumulated enough that it began to crunch under my boots, my breath puffing in the air in front of me. It was getting cold enough that staying out in the open would quickly become a real danger.

I kept my eyes fixed forward on the trail, following its winding path up the hill.

Right in the middle of my trek, Buddy let out a sudden and sharp bark before tearing off ahead.

"Bud!" I shouted, watching him disappear over the horizon. "Where the hell are you going?"

I picked up the pace, moving into a jog as I hurried after my dog. He wasn't the sort to get distracted by a rabbit or some such nonsense, he was too well-trained for that. Another bark cut through the air as I continued on as fast as I could.

"I'm coming!" I called out.

I reached the top of the slope, my lungs burning from the run and the cold air.

That's when I spotted her.

She was curled up on the forest floor, her body covered in a fine layer of snow. She was still, her legs flopped over to one side and her arm draped over her chest.

"Ah, shit."

I hurried over and dropped down to my knees, slipping my hand slowly and carefully behind her head. As I turned her toward me, it was impossible not to notice right away how damned beautiful she was.

Her beauty was striking, in fact. It was enough to make the windy, snowy and cold world around me vanish. Her face was heart-shaped, with delicate cheekbones, a pert chin, and a small nose. Her lips were so damn full and ripe that all I could think about was kissing them, as insane as that might've been to think about in a situation like that.

I shook my head, coming back to the moment and focused on the important matter before me. It was hard to tell her age for certain, but I guessed that she was somewhere in her mid-twenties. She was slender and slight, her jeans clinging to her curves and pulling my attention back to things that I shouldn't have been thinking about. But damn if she wasn't a beauty.

A bit of blood seeped from the back of her head, the scalp red and raised. I only knew basic first-aid, but it didn't take a damn doctor to put together what might've happened. The horse was probably hers and got spooked somehow, tossing her off and giving her head a nasty knock. She was still alive, her chest rising and falling at a steady, slow pace. In her gloved hand was a phone, the screen cracked beyond use or repair. All the same, I took it and tucked it into my back pocket.

I stood and glanced to the right at Wheeler Ranch down below in the valley. There was a possibility that the girl was from there although there was no way to know for sure. Even if she was, the ranch was miles away. Not a good idea to hoof it down the mountain carrying her in the inclement weather. Besides, my truck wasn't far.

"What do you think, Buddy?" I asked, giving the girl a once-over. "Up for some company?" Once the girl woke up and told me who she was and where she was from, I'd take her home straightaway.

Buddy barked, as if giving his approval of my decision. I lived alone—aside from Buddy, of course. I liked it that way. Didn't need company, especially after the kind of life I'd lived. All the same, there wasn't a chance in hell I'd leave someone unconscious out in the cold.

I bent down, scooping the girl off the ground. She was light as a feather, and I was able to fireman carry her with no problem.

"Back to the car, big guy!" I called out to Buddy. "Get a move on!"

My dog wasted no time taking off into the woods, staying within eyesight as I carried her through the snow. The temperature dropped lower as we made our way, the snow accumulating by the second.

I held the mystery woman against me, her body curled into mine. She was still warm, her shearling-lined coat soft. Even though I was focused on getting her to safety, it was impossible not to notice her scent, the way she felt in my arms. I pushed that out of my thoughts as best I could, focusing instead on bracing against the cold and wind, and completing the task at hand.

It took about ten minutes of trudging through the woods until I was able to spot my truck, the '95 cherry-red Ford F-150 that I'd been driving for the last few decades. Like me, she was getting up in years. But also like me, she still knew how to work her butt off.

Buddy was already there, waiting patiently at the truck's side. I approached, opening the door of the extended cab and gently laying the girl down. Once she was taken care of, I opened the passenger-side door for Buddy. Seconds later, I was inside, the engine growling to life and heat flowing out of the vents. Relief took hold at knowing the girl was safe and warm for the time being, but there was still the matter of getting her home.

The Ford handled the snow like a champ, the old girl barreling and rumbling over the rough forest floor.

My place was a little ways off, but it wouldn't take long to get there. As I glanced at the beauty in my backseat, I started wondering what the hell I'd gotten myself into.

CHAPTER 3

BETH

I let out a groan as I rolled over, pain pounding through my head. As I came back to the world of the living, the repetitive, wet press of what I knew right away was a tongue caused my eyes to snap open. I groaned and rolled again, this time to the other side. The licking stopped for a moment, then started again.

A warm, toasty fire crackled in the big, wooden fireplace in front of me, the heat heaven on my skin. But the licking was what really captured my attention. I sat halfway up, another blast of pain coursing through my head as I looked around.

"What the hell?"

My vision was blurred, but it cleared up by the second, enough to see a dog, its tongue lolling out of its mouth. The dog backed up, as if it had done something wrong. It was beautiful—a big, strong animal with a gorgeous coat of black, white and yellow fur. The poor pup appeared so chastened by my outburst that I couldn't help but feel a little bad.

"Sorry, boy. Or, ah, girl."

The dog responded by cocking its head to the side, partially in confusion, partially as if trying to size me up. Although the animal was big and powerful looking, it didn't strike me as dangerous.

Danger. The word stuck in my head, the situation I was in suddenly dawning on me. I bolted up into a full sitting position, the shock at my surroundings enough to make me ignore the pain thumping in my head. I wasn't at home, that was for damn sure. I was on a couch in the living room of a small but cozy cabin. Before me was a roaring fire, a kitchen off to my left. A Dutch oven was on the stove, a small fire lit e beneath it, delicious smells flowing into the room.

A small hallway led to two more rooms, one of which I guessed was the bedroom of whoever owned the place. The cabin's windows looked out onto the woods, revealing snow coming down in sheets.

My heart beat faster, and I tried to remember what had happened. All that came to mind was the snow and Margo and... everything after that was a blur.

The dog whined as if it were trying to get my attention.

"What's up, pup?"

The dog let out another whine, turning to the couch's end table. I pushed off the big, heavy blanket that was on top of me and leaned over to see where the pup was trying to direct my attention. I spotted my phone right away.

I shot my hand out and snatched it off the end table. The screen was totally smashed, the body itself cracked from top to bottom on the back. Even though I could see that the phone was nothing but a piece of useless junk in my hand, I still tried to turn it on. Nothing appeared on the screen, of course.

I let the hand holding the phone drop limply into my lap. As I did, I spotted something else on the end table—a note. Desperate for any clue as to where I was, I grabbed the piece of loose-leaf paper and read. The handwriting was simple and clean, all lines and angles; a man's handwriting I guessed.

You took a tumble. As you can see, your phone's no good. I stepped out to take care of some things around the property. When I get back, we'll talk about getting you home.

– Jack

P.S. Dog's name is Buddy. Don't be afraid to give him a pet or two.

Jack. I set the piece of paper back on the table. Everything seemed so surreal. The cabin was very simple, without much in the way of décor aside from a few rugs here and there. A pair of tall, wooden bookshelves were against the wall, packed with colorful spines. The place was neat and tidy, homey even, in spite of its sparse interior.

I wanted to know who this Jack guy was, and if he was any danger to me. The fact that he'd left a note and made sure to address the matter of me getting home was some relief—it meant he knew I'd be worried when I woke up.

I turned my attention to the dog, who was still in front of me seated on his back paws, as if waiting for an order.

"Buddy, huh?" I asked.

I reached forward and pet the top of his head, Buddy closing his eyes and letting his tongue hang out in pure bliss.

My head still hurt like hell, but all the same, I wanted to find out what I could about where I was, and who this Jack guy might be. I threw the blanket off me and stood up. The moment I was on my feet however, I realized that I'd risen far faster than I should've. The world spun for a moment, and I had to blink hard a few times before I was steady again. Buddy hurried to my side, looking up at me with eyes that seemed full of concern.

"Wow." I placed my hand on my head. "I really did a number on my noggin."

More memories of the fall came back—the sighting of the bear, Margo's sprint down the path. My heart skipped a beat at the thought of Margo being alone out in the cold. But I knew the girl well enough to know that there was a good chance she'd bolted right back down the trail and toward the ranch.

Mom and Dad. God, they were probably worried sick about me if Margo showed up without me. I looked around for a clock, spotting an old-fashioned—analog one over the fireplace. It was a little after two, which meant that I'd been out for about two hours. My parents were probably frantic. I needed to get ahold of them soon and let them know I was alright.

"OK, buddy," I said. "Guess the next step is figuring out where the hell your owner is."

Buddy barked as I stood there trying to figure out my next move, then hurried over to one of the nearby windows and put his paws up on the sill. He let out another bark as he looked out of the window, his eyes on something, or someone.

I went over to join him. When I reached the window, I noticed that the pain in my head had subsided a little. The grogginess I'd been dealing with since waking up faded by the moment, and I was slowly but surely beginning to feel normal again.

Once at the window, I looked out to see more of my surroundings, trying to get my bearings of where I was. The cabin was situated in the middle of a small clearing, a steep incline covered in trees just beyond. The pines and aspens towered high over the cabin, the greens of their branches now heavy with snow.

It wasn't the foliage that I was focused on, however. Emerging from the thickness of the trees was a massive, broad-shouldered man, his powerful form reminding me of the stature of the trees he walked among. Between the snow and his bundled clothes, I couldn't make much out as far as his features were concerned, other than that he was tall and bearded, an axe slung over his shoulder.

I would've thought that the sight of a strange man approaching me in the middle of the woods with a freaking axe might cause some distress. However, there was something about the way he carried himself that put me at ease.

I watched as he made his way over toward what appeared to be a storage shed. He pulled open the door, a small cascade of snow falling from the structure's roof. He entered, emerging without the axe.

It was impossible to take my eyes off of him. His movements were confident and powerful, fluid and effortless. As he made his way around the property, he seemed a man in his element.

"Jack," I said softly, repeating the name I'd read on the note.

After a few more minutes of handling odds and ends, he entered the shed once more, coming out with a big bundle of firewood tucked underneath his arm. This time, he approached the cabin.

I gasped, realizing that he was about to come in and see me staring at him like some kind of creeper. I sprang from where I was near the window, making my way back over to the couch. Buddy came with me, curling up at my feet as if doing his part to create the illusion that I'd been there the whole time.

Once I was seated on the couch, the big, comfy blanket wrapped around me, the door opened. Tension tied my stomach in knots as cold air rushed into the house, a few curls of snow whipping around the man's huge, hulking figure.

I'd noticed his stature when I'd first seen him outside, but up close and personal, his sheer size struck me. He had to have been around six-feet, six-inches tall, nearly needing to duck his head to enter the cabin.

I tried to take in as many details as I could without staring. He pulled off his black beanie, uncovering a head of dark, wavy hair with gray threaded throughout, his thick beard the same color. His eyes were a striking bright blue. He took off his coat revealing a dark blue flannel shirt and rugged jeans, a pair of well-worn work boots on his feet. Even in his warm, loose-fitting clothing, I could see that his body was big and powerful, with broad shoulders and strong hands. He set the cord of firewood down, rolling his shoulders once his arms were free.

He cleared his throat as he shook off the light dusting of snow, hanging up his hat and coat and stomping his boots on the mat to clear off whatever might've been sticking to them.

"Buddy?" his voice was deep and booming, so much so I could practically feel it in my bones. He looked up, his ice-blue eyes flashing.

As he scanned the cabin for his dog, I noticed something else about him—he was much older than me. It was hard to guess his age exactly but I figured somewhere in his mid-forties, maybe even closer to fifty.

Even so, he was insanely attractive. Jack pulled off his gloves and I found myself staring at his big, rough hands, my pussy clenching as I imagined them touching my body.

Jack put his eyes on me, and being pinned by his piercing blues made me feel like I was in the spotlight.

"You're up."

It wasn't a question but more of a statement. All the same, I couldn't help but respond.

"Yeah. Sort of."

He raised one of his thick, dark eyebrows. "Sort of?"

I smiled weakly. "Just still feels like I'm in a fog."

Jack nodded, understanding what I was getting at.

"After a fall like that, I'm sure it does." He craned his head, spotting Buddy over on the floor near my feet. "What's the story, big guy? Too lazy to come say hi?" Jack stepped over, a small, but warm smile on his face as he reached down to give Buddy a pet on the head. "Or maybe just too comfy."

After he'd said his hellos to Buddy, Jack stepped back a few feet away from me. Between his note and his body language, there was no doubt that he was conscious of how disorienting and potentially even scary the situation could be for me.

He rolled up his sleeves and crossed his arms, his forearms beautifully thick and toned and covered in just the right amount of hair. The fire crackled behind him. Even though all he was doing was standing there, I couldn't ignore how strangely attracted to him I was.

Nor could I ignore the way he looked at me. It was as if he were annoyed by the dumb, clueless girl who he'd had to take care of.

"So, let's get you caught up." He held up his palm. "You're about five miles from Wheeler Hill, where I found you after you took a nasty spill and knocked your head."

"Margo." The name shot out of my mouth.

"Margo." He was confused at first, then nodded in understanding. "Your horse."

"Is she OK? Was she hurt?" I looked around the cabin, realizing how silly it was for me to be scanning the place as if I might spot Margo hiding behind a bookshelf.

"Only saw traces of her. Margo's how I knew to look for you. I spotted her running down the path with a saddle but no rider. Unfortunately, I can only guess where she might've gone after that."

"Home. She knows where to go."

"And where might home be?" Right after he asked the question, he held up his palm, as if he'd remembered something. "You want some tea?" He gestured toward the kitchen where a stainless-steel tea kettle sat on the stove next to the Dutch oven that contained whatever smelled so damn good.

He didn't wait for me to respond before heading over and grabbing a couple of mugs from the cupboard. Already I was getting the impression that this Jack was someone who did whatever he wanted, and everyone else was just along for the ride.

"Uh, sure."

I kept my eyes on him as he prepared the tea, placing a bag in each mug and turning on the gas burner under the kettle. Maybe it was a little silly to think that this guy might slip me something, but hell, I had no idea who he was, what he might want with me.

"Before I tell you where home is, I need to know if you've got any way of communicating outside of this place."

Once more, an annoyed expression flashed on his face. It didn't last long, however, as if he sensed that my request was more than reasonable.

"Your phone's wrecked, as I'm sure you saw. But you

can use mine." Once the fire was going under the kettle, he stepped over to his coat and pulled his phone out, tossing it over to me.

I caught it, noticing right away that it wasn't exactly the latest phone model. In fact, I'd never seen a phone like it in my life. It flipped open and didn't have a touchscreen. Moreover, it looked like it'd seen far, far better days.

"How the hell do you use this thing?"

He chuckled. "Open it up and type. I know you kids halfway expect your phones these days to chew your food for you, but I'm sure you'll figure it out."

There was that condescension again. Part of me wanted to roll my eyes at his comment, but a greater part wanted to simply get in touch with my parents and let them know I was alright.

"You're not going to get any reception worth a damn on that phone. Nothing good enough for a call, that is. Stick to texting."

I nodded. It took me a minute to figure out how to use the phone keypad to navigate the simple, black-and-white menu. Once I got the hang of it, I opened up the text message window and sent one to Mom's number, telling her that I was fine, that I was in a cabin a few miles west of the ranch, that I'd get home as soon as I could, and to text, not call.

Relief washed over me as I hit send, an old-school animation of a letter growing wings and shooting off into the distance appearing on the screen.

"Where'd you get this thing anyway?" I asked. "The natural history museum?"

He let out a wry chuckle as he eased down into the chair across from the couch.

"You live out here in the woods for a time and let me

know how that eleven-hundred-dollar piece of glass works out for you. Hell, you've got proof on the table right there." He nodded to my ruined phone.

I took one more look at his phone, noting how worn and beat up it was. I didn't want to pry, but it appeared to be at least a decade old.

"Dropped that more times than I can count," he said as he reached over for the phone. "Built like a tank. You live the life that I do out here in the woods, you might want something like that for your next phone."

There was once more a trace of condescension in his voice, that "explaining things to a dumb kid" tinge to his words. His eyes said something different, however. There was heat to his gaze that I couldn't quite read.

He let out an amused snort, glancing down at his phone and breaking eye contact between us.

"It's your lucky day, reception's good enough for a response. Half the time I need to go into town to use this thing." He tossed the phone back over and I neatly caught it, checking the screen to see that there was a message from Mom.

She wanted to know exactly where I was, who I was with, and if I was hurt. And she let me know that Margo had come back fine, though a tad shaken up.

"I need to get back," I said, lifting my eyes from the phone. "My parents are probably worried out of their minds."

"Well, they're going to have to wait. There's not a chance in hell I'm driving out in this mess." He nodded toward the snow coming down in big, fat flakes and whipping around in the gusty wind.

"Don't you have, I don't know, chains you could put on your tires or something?"

Another dismissive snort. "That might work when you want to drive from that fancy-ass ranch of yours into town to grab some pizza, but not when you're out in the hinterlands like I am." He leaned forward, clasping his hands. "You *are* from Wheeler Ranch, right?"

I felt a touch defensive, as if it might not be a good idea to come forward with such information.

"What makes you think that?"

"Well, first the fact that you were near it. Second..." he looked me up and down. "The fact that you *look* the type to live at a place like that."

"What's that supposed to mean?"

Another chuckle, as if he were more amused by my outburst than anything else.

"I'm no fashion expert, but I've seen the kind of boots you've got on—they're not cheap. Not to mention that fine horse you were riding."

I crossed my arms. "What difference does it make if my family comes from money?"

The whistle of the tea kettle cut me off.

"Keep talking," he said as he rose and started in the direction of the kitchen.

I waited for him to take the screaming thing off the burner before starting again.

"What difference does it make if my family comes from money?"

He said nothing at first, instead focusing on pouring the hot water over the tea bags, as if we were on *his* time when it came to answering questions. Jack came back over, handing me a steaming mug.

When he was settled back in his chair, all nice and comfy, he answered my question.

"Oh, it doesn't make any difference, I suppose. Though

it does give an insight into how you might've ended up ass-over-teakettle, so to speak, in the middle of a blizzard."

I was offended. I didn't quite know what to say.

"Are you suggesting that I'm some silly rich girl who doesn't know her way around her horse?"

"Nah, you seem to know your way around; all the way around, to be specific."

A tinge of anger flashed through me. "Listen, thanks for saving me and all that, but you don't have to be a jerk."

He offered a small, wry smirk in response. I'd only known Jack for a short time, but he was already confusing me. He was gruff, but there was a bit of sardonic humor to his personality. I didn't know what to make of him, and the fact that it was impossible to ignore how hot he was only complicated matters.

Jack reached forward, grabbing the firewood poker and giving the burning wood a prod. Embers flew up, whooshing and rushing into the air.

"Gotta throw some more on. Gimme a sec."

He stood, making his way over to the pile of chopped wood he'd brought in. As he stoked the fire, I found myself thinking about this strange man with whom I was snowed in. Namely, what the hell was his story?

If I had to guess on the type of man who'd choose to live alone out in the middle of the woods, I'd assume that there was something wrong with him, that he was weird or strange. Jack, kinda dickish though he might've been, didn't seem that way at all. Then again, it wasn't as though I'd known him for very long.

"Well, you and I are going to be here for at least the night. My place isn't much, but it's either here or freezing your ass off in the woods. Take your pick."

He walked over to the kitchen and I watched as he

lifted the lid of the Dutch oven, holding his nose over the contents. I couldn't tell exactly what it was, but it smelled like some kind of stew. The pain from the fall and the fear of waking in a strange place were fading by the moment, hunger replacing them.

"What is that over there?"

"Stew."

He said nothing else, and for a moment I found myself wondering if he'd picked up on the subtext of my asking the question.

"Don't worry," he said. "You can have some."

My mouth watered. I watched as he lifted the lid of a nearby breadbasket, taking out a half loaf of dark bread. With fluid movements, he placed the bread onto a sheet and put it into the oven.

"I mean, you don't *have* to give me any." Part of me didn't want to impose, while another part of me didn't want him to think he was doing me any favors.

He chuckled, shaking his head as if he saw right through me. "Didn't plan on you being here tonight, but you're a guest all the same. You want food, you've got it. There's beer too if you're in the mood."

My mouth watered all over again. After the kind of day I'd had, a beer sounded like heaven. Another glance over at Jack, however, made me reconsider. Last thing I wanted was to lose my inhibitions and give in to something I ought not to.

It didn't take long before he stepped over to the small, round table by the window, setting two places for us, putting down bowls, silverware, and bread and butter.

"We're ready. Come on over."

I rose, another wave of unsteadiness running through me, probably the last traces of the effects from the fall. I was fine, but all the same Jack bolted over with surprising speed for a man his size. He placed one hand on my shoulder, the other on the small of my back.

"You alright?"

The unsteadiness was replaced by something else—a rush of feelings at his nearness. His touch, his smell, the flash of his ice-blue eyes... they were damn near irresistible. My heart raced faster, my pussy clenching once again.

"I'm fine. Just a little dizzy."

He gave me a quick look up and down to make sure that I really was fine before taking his huge hand from my shoulder and stepping back.

"Careful now. Got a feeling you're tougher than you look, but all the same, you took a hell of a tumble."

"Tougher than I look? What's that supposed to mean?" I smiled slightly at his words.

"You went out in the middle of a snowstorm," he said, going over to the table and nodding for me to join him. "That takes some nerve."

I went over to the table and he pulled out a chair for me. I normally wasn't one to go for old-school chivalry, but there was something about Jack that made me not mind. I sat down, the rich, thick stew making me even hungrier than I was before. There was hot bread and fresh butter, and Jack brought over a can of cold beer that he poured evenly into both of our glasses. I sipped my tea as I watched him finish, the warm liquid settling in my belly.

"So," he said, sliding into his seat. "You've got me at a disadvantage. My name's Jack, but I don't know yours."

"Elizabeth," I said. "But everyone calls me Beth."

He raised his cup of beer. "Well, cheers, Beth."

"Cheers."

We tapped our glasses, Jack glancing down at his food. "Alright, dig in."

My stomach rumbled. Instead of eating, however, I found myself staring at Jack as he readied to take a bite.

I was feeling very hungry—in more ways than one.

CHAPTER 4

JACK

Goddamn, was it hard to keep myself in check.
Put yourself in her shoes. She's in some stranger's house in the middle of the woods. You're lucky she didn't mace you the second you greeted her. Doesn't help matters that you're as grouchy as they come.

My inner monologue tempered the heat I felt for her but only a little. Truth was that it'd been hard as hell not pouncing on Beth like one of the wild animals that roamed the woods outside my cabin. Maybe it was my imagination, but I could've sworn by the way she glanced at me out of the corner of her eye that she felt the same way.

I watched as she took one bite of stew, then another, then another. No doubt her apprehension was fading and her appetite returning.

"Easy now," I said. "Eat too much of that too fast and you'll be paying for it with a bellyache."

Beth flicked her eyes up at me, as if her first instinct might've been to tell me to mind my own damn business, that she'd eat how she wanted to. I could already sense in the little bit of time we'd known each other that she was a strong-willed woman who didn't appreciate anyone telling her what to do.

She didn't sass me back, however. Instead, she slowly set down her spoon and washed her bite down with a slow sip of beer.

"It's good," she said. "What's the meat?"

I lifted the wooden spoon, a huge chunk of rich meat pooled in gravy on the end.

"That right there's venison."

She offered a small, wry smile in response. "Let me guess—you shot it, cut it, cleaned it, and cooked it yourself."

"Nope," I said. "Actually, got it at Trader Joe's."

Beth cocked her head to the side, as if not sure what to make of my comment. When she realized I was messing around, she allowed herself a small laugh.

"For a guy who lives alone in the woods, you have a surprising sense of humor."

"Well, I can cover myself in dirt and speak in grunts if that'd be more what you're expecting."

"I didn't mean anything by it," she said. "More that... well, when I stand on the top of Wheeler Hill and look out over the forest, spot all the little plumes of smoke coming out of the woods, I imagine what the guys who live out there might be like."

"Guys?" I asked. "More than a few women out here—some of the toughest I've ever met in my life, in fact. We're equal-opportunity hermits, you know."

She laughed. "Well, man or woman, I always wondered what kind of person would live out here all alone."

"I can't speak for all of them but the ones I've met are just like me. They want peace and solitude. No cities, no high-rises, no traffic, no Netflix."

"No Netflix?" she asked with a smile of her own. "Guess that means I won't ask what you've been streaming as part of our dinner conversation."

I let out a dry laugh. "People have their reasons for living out here. And I don't pry. That's a mutual understanding between our kind."

"So, why are *you* out here? What's your story?"

"I just said. Peace and solitude."

My words carried an edge that seemed to chasten her a bit. Her eyes fell down to her stew.

"You don't need to be a dick about it."

Maybe she was right about that. All the same, my past was my past, and I didn't have the slightest urge to share it with anyone, let alone some random woman who'd ended up in my cabin during the middle of a damn snowstorm.

I turned my eyes to the window, watching the snow come down hard. Part of me had hoped the torrential weather wouldn't live up to the hype the weather people had been dishing out over the last day. The darkness of the sky and the piled up inches on my truck, however, made it clear that we were in for a heavy downfall.

Beth turned her attention to the nearby bookshelf.

"*Don Quixote*," she said with a small smile. "Love that one."

"You've read it?"

"That surprise you?"

"Well, yeah. Nothing personal, but most people can barely get through half a sentence before taking out their phone, let alone reading an entire book."

She laughed in a way that made it clear she agreed with me. "You're not wrong about that. And truth be told, it was a while ago that I read it, all the way back in elementary school. I always called my friend Jamie 'Pancho' because I liked to imagine her as my sidekick. She wasn't crazy about the nickname."

After she spoke, she took a long look around the cabin.

"God, this must be the perfect place to read. Total heaven to be able to sit by the fire with a glass of wine, listening to the crackle and watching the snow come down as you sink into a book, warm pup at your feet."

"That's how I'd been planning on spending the evening, as a matter of fact."

She pursed her lips. "Until you had an unexpected visitor, that is."

I chuckled, shaking my head and taking another bite of my stew. Beth smiled back, dipping a butter-covered piece of bread into her bowl then tossing it into her mouth.

"I may like my quiet, but I wasn't going to leave you out there to freeze to death."

"See?" she asked. "I knew there was a soft heart underneath that gruff exterior."

She was joking but I couldn't help but think about how goddamn little someone would have to know about me to suggest I had anything like a "soft heart." If only she knew where I'd come from…

"Let's not go crazy," I said.

Beth glanced out the window. "What a mess out there. What do you do here when there's that much snow? Hole up for a few weeks?"

I shrugged. "It's been done before. Last year when that winter storm hit, I stayed in the cabin for a good twenty days, just Buddy and me and my books."

She arched her eyebrows. "Wow. I like my peace, but that's another level."

"Not for me. But to answer your question, I can leave

whenever I want. Got solid tires on that truck, and a plow in the storage shed that I mount on front. Easy as pie to get through just about anything Mother Nature throws at me. I didn't stay because I was stuck, I stayed because I wanted to."

She took another bite, washing it down with a small sip of beer. I could tell she was being careful about how much she drank, trying to stay in control.

"Sounds kind of fun." Beth glanced away, giving the matter more thought. "Actually, I *can* see the appeal of being out here in the middle of nowhere all alone except for a cool dog. You've got a cozy little cabin, beer, and a fireplace." She squinted her eyes and gave me a knowing look. "I bet you've got a big freezer out back just stocked full of food, probably gas and a generator too."

I chuckled. "Enough supplies for three months."

She sighed, shaking her head as if now living in the fantasy of the scenario.

"I get it. I mean, not having to worry about getting small business loans and renting office space and networking and trying to break into a new business and all the things that come along with it..."

Beth was speaking at a mile a minute, the words tumbling out of her mouth. I couldn't help but laugh.

"Sounds stressful."

"Nah. Just a lot to do. No big deal."

There was no doubt in my mind that whatever it was, it was a big deal—maybe the most important thing in her life. All the same, I didn't like it when people pried into my life, so I extended the same courtesy to her. Not to mention that I wasn't all that keen on playing therapist.

We ate and drank, the stew and beer and buttered bread

filling me up in just the right way. When I was done, I leaned back and put my hands on my belly.

"That enough for you?" I asked.

"That has to be the most filling meal I've had in months."

"That right? I'd guess the eating would be good over there on Wheeler Ranch."

"It's not that. Mom and Dad are always trying to get me to sit down and eat a meal. It's just that I'm the type who gets busy and you know, forgets to eat."

"Well, no need for that here. You want anything else, just let me know."

As I said the words, a strange glimmer appeared in her eye, as if there was something else on her mind. The way her lip curled slightly made me wonder if it was food she was thinking about.

Didn't matter. Beth was about the sexiest damn woman I'd laid eyes on in as long as I could remember. And the idea of climbing under the covers with her and taking in the sight of that assuredly beautiful body was enough to make me solid as a stone. Getting involved with her would surely become complicated—my life out in the woods was all about avoiding just that.

"Hey!" Beth called out to me as I made my way to the sink.

I glanced over my shoulder. "Yeah?"

"Those dishes, let me help you with them. You cooked, after all."

I set the dishes down next to the sink. "Nah, don't worry about that. You're a guest here. Not to mention, you need to be getting all the rest you can."

She let out a *pssh* as she stood up, picking up the remaining dishes on the table and bringing them over.

"I just bonked my head, I'm not totally helpless. And besides, if you're going to be letting me stay here for the night, I want to pitch in and make myself useful."

The firm, insistent tone of her voice made it clear that it'd be more effort to talk her out of it than to simply let her help.

"Fine. But this isn't the biggest kitchen in the world, so try not to get in the way."

She flashed me another charming smile as she stepped over to join me.

"Don't worry, I'm small."

"Small enough that I could toss your butt to the other side of the room if you mess with my process."

Her eyes flashed at my words, as if the idea of me handling her in that way was somewhat appealing. Hell, maybe it was. Beth wasn't tiny, I'd guess around five-feet, seven-inches. But just about any woman was small compared to me. The way she looked at me made me imagine putting my hands on her, ripping off those clothes and climbing on top, spreading her legs and taking my cock into my hand and—

"Got any gloves?"

Her words snapped me back into the moment.

"Huh? Gloves?"

"You know, rubber gloves. The kind you wear when washing dishes?"

"Don't really use those," I said, stepping in front of the sink, preparing to get started.

She scoffed and smiled. "Figures that an oh-so-manly man like you wouldn't care about wrecking your hands with dish soap."

"With all I do with these," I said, holding up my hands. "A little dish soap isn't going to make a difference."

Beth said nothing. Her eyes fixed onto my hands as if she were starting to get some ideas of her own about what I could do with them. Tension gathered in the air around us, my heart beating a bit faster.

"Shit, you know what?" As soon as I spoke the words, Beth turned her head as if coming to her senses. "I think I do have some gloves after all."

I dropped into a squat, opening the cabinet doors underneath the sink and taking a gander. Sure enough, a pair of unused rubber gloves were in there. I grabbed them and rose to my feet.

"Here. Think they came with a package of cleaner or something. Never been used."

Beth smiled, plucking the gloves from my hand and putting them on.

"There we go. Now, we'll both clean and after, we'll compare. Bet you anything my hands will be much nicer."

I smirked as I grabbed a sponge. "That's because you've got the hands of a Denver girl. Those tend to be nice and dainty."

"Take a lot of Denver girls' hands?" she asked.

I laughed. "Pleading the fifth on that one."

With that, we went to work. Took a little getting used to someone cleaning next to me; like everything else around the cabin, doing dishes was typically a one-man operation. To my surprise, it didn't take long before we had a well-oiled routine going. In fact, the whole process took a lot less time than me doing it on my own.

We were very near each other as we worked, our elbows bumping and her scent drifting up to me, Beth allowing the occasional smile as we cracked jokes with one another.

It was hard not to notice how nice it was to have her

there. Strange, because never in a million years did I think some random woman intruding on my solitude during a snowstorm would brighten my mood in the slightest.

When we were done, the dishes set on the drying rack, Beth turned and leaned against the counter, letting out a sigh of relief.

"You know what? I think we deserve a little reward after all that hard work."

"What'd you have in mind?"

She narrowed her eyes and pursed her lips, giving the matter some serious consideration.

"You ask me, I think a little something sweet would do the trick." She turned her head toward me. "But something tells me you're not a sweet tooth sort of guy."

"You'd be right about that. But… hmm…"

I stepped over to the fridge and opened it. I spotted one ingredient and then another, a small smile forming on my face as the plan came together.

"You in the mood for a little Irish?" I asked, pulling a bottle of Bailey's down from my liquor shelf. "Not a lot, just enough to make it interesting."

She grinned. "Depends on what *it* is, I suppose."

"Dessert. But I don't want to ruin the surprise."

Her grin grew wider. "Sure. I love a good surprise."

I watched as she bounded over to the couch, her fluid movements both appealing to the eye and giving me an indication that her injuries weren't too serious. Beth plopped onto the couch, pulling the blanket over as Buddy curled up at her feet, her eyes on the crackling fire.

I went to it, taking out milk, heavy cream and cocoa powder, pouring what I needed into a medium-sized bowl and whisking it. Didn't take long before I had some good-looking whipped cream going. I heated the milk and cocoa powder—and a small splash of Bailey's, of course—on the stove, pouring the concoction into two ceramic mugs and topping it with whipped cream.

Once they were ready, I brought them over, sitting down next to Beth on the couch and passing her a mug.

"Is this... hot chocolate?"

"Sure is. Had a little cocoa powder left over from when I made mole sauce a while back. It's not a hot fudge sundae, but it should satisfy your sweet tooth."

She brought the mug to her lips and sipped, leaving a small dab of whipped cream on her nose. Beth giggled, dabbing it off and popping her finger into her mouth, wrapping her lips around it. It took all the restraint I had to push the dirty thoughts out of my head.

"Good stuff?"

"Not bad at all." She took another sip before lowering her mug, giving me an odd, cock-eyed sort of look.

"Now what's that expression all about?"

"Nothing. Just thinking about how for a guy who lives alone in the woods, you're pretty normal all things considered."

I let out a quick bark of a laugh. "Hell of a compliment. I do believe they refer to those as the backhanded kind."

She smiled. "Not how I meant it. I mean, you're pretty gruff and all, but there's something else to you."

I wanted her to leave it there. The longer she spoke, the more I began to feel like she was on the verge of asking me just what had brought me to my current way of living. *That* was a subject most assuredly off-limits.

She shook her head. "Really, more than anything, you're kind enough to let me stay here."

MY EX'S DAD | 43

Funny word, *kind*. Couldn't imagine many people who'd consider me anything close to that.

"And to top it all off, you make a pretty darn good hot chocolate."

I sipped my own mug. The drink was creamy and sweet and just the right amount of boozy. As I'd told Beth, I'd never been a sweet tooth kind of guy, but even I had to admit that it was pretty damn tasty.

"Wait," she said, her eyes flicking down. "I forgot to ask you about your hands."

"My what?"

"Your hands. Remember? You were so certain that the gloves didn't matter. Let me check them and find out." She set down her mug on the coffee table and reached over.

Before I had a chance to say anything, she took my right hand into hers. I set down my mug as she rubbed my palm, her eyes looking up toward the ceiling. The sensation of her skin on mine was intoxicating. My cock stiffened in my jeans, my blood pumping. The attraction I'd felt for Beth since spotting her in the woods came rushing back.

"Yep, just like I thought, incredibly dry." She laughed. "Maybe I can thank you for this by taking you into town and getting you a manicure."

I snorted. "Not a chance in hell. And I didn't do what I did because I wanted a thank you." I glanced down at her hand. "Let me see yours. How am I supposed to know my skin is dry if I don't have anything to compare it to?"

"Fair enough." Beth stuck out her hand to me, her fingers long, her skin no doubt soft.

I took her hand into mine, the attraction and electricity returning with even more intensity than before.

"What do you think?" she asked with a sly smile.

I lifted my eyes to hers, her expression softening into

something sultrier, something that made it clear to me that she had the same thing on her mind that I did.

I couldn't resist her any longer. I leaned in, placing my hand behind her head and gently guiding her lips to mine. She didn't resist one bit, the flavor of chocolate still lingering on her tongue as we kissed.

CHAPTER 5

BETH

The kiss was unexpected.

Well, maybe not totally. I'd been thinking about Jack in that way since laying eyes on him. Gruff and kind of a dick as he might've been, the more I'd gotten to know him, the more I wanted him.

His musk was the first thing I noticed as he kissed me, that inviting, warm scent that reminded me of nature itself wrapping around me as surely as his big arms were wrapped around my waist. I let out a soft moan as we kissed, my lips parting and his tongue finding mine, the fire crackling in the background.

Between the man, the fire, the snow and the cozy cabin setting, it was perfect.

His taste washed over me, the sweetness of the Bailey's lingering on his lips. The more I kissed him, the more I wanted, and as his hand moved up my thigh between my legs, all I could do was squirm in anticipation.

A low growl sounded out as he kissed me hard, putting his hand on the small of my back and guiding me to lay down. Jack positioned himself over top of me, his massive, powerful body blocking out everything else. His mouth fell onto the slope of my neck, the wetness and softness of his lips blending with the rough bristle of his beard.

When he reached my face again, he paused and lifted his head up. An expression of concern painted his features.

"Something wrong?" I asked. It took a hell of a lot of effort to focus enough to speak. By that point I was so turned on that I could hardly think straight, my panties about soaked through.

He kept those gorgeous blue eyes fixed on mine.

"This is all pretty damn sudden. You want it to happen, it happens. But if you want it to stop right now, it stops."

He was giving me an out. I couldn't help but smile at his words.

"No, I don't want it to stop. In fact, I can't wait to see how far it goes."

Jack grinned. "Good. Because I've got some ideas..."

He lowered himself again, his lips pressing against my mouth and his hardness against my thigh. I moaned through the kiss, opening my legs and wrapping them around his waist, his cock now pressing against my sensitive center through my jeans.

He hadn't even taken a single article of clothing off and already he was making me feel all kinds of good.

He continued to press his stiff cock against me, grinding his no doubt huge manhood against my pussy. We continued to kiss, his hands moving down to the hem of my shirt and reaching underneath, his rough, warm touch traveling over my middle all the way to my bra.

I did the same, reaching under his flannel and placing my hands on the flat plane of his abs. Even without seeing them I could tell they were chiseled. That sexy as hell happy trail was the perfect amount of hair.

The longer we kissed, the more Jack seemed to become possessed by an animal-like passion, his hands reaching underneath my bra and teasing my nipples, pinning me down just the way I wanted. When I couldn't take any more, I grabbed his shirt and eagerly pulled it off, revealing his torso underneath.

Jack's body was even more stunning than I imagined. His chest was huge and solid, two square pecs dusted with the perfect amount of salt and pepper hair. His shoulders were broad and round, the wide upper V of his chest and back tapering down into a slimmer, but just as solid middle. His arms were thick, his biceps tense from the strain of holding his body up.

Damn. This life of his out in the woods is treating him well.

As I lay there eye-fucking him, Jack reached down and took hold of my shirt pulling it up slowly. I arched my back a bit, the soft material sliding across my skin and then finally over my head. My hands went to work on my button and fly, and I quickly shimmied out of my pants and kicked them off.

I didn't have on anything particularly sexy; I hadn't expected to be partaking in any sort of bedroom shenanigans. My bra was a simple black sports bra, my panties matching and high-cut. But the way Jack looked at me, you would've thought I'd had on the most tantalizing underthings imaginable.

He looked me up and down with hungry eyes, shaking his head as if he couldn't believe what he was seeing. I could feel the heat of his barely restrained desire.

I wanted him desperately to do more than just look.

"Goddamn, you're something else."

As I grinned, I swept my eyes over his body, my gaze

lingering on the bits of gray here and there on his chest and in his beard. They were a reminder of something I'd nearly forgotten—the age difference. Was I really about to sleep with a man who was old enough to be my father?

The moment he placed his hands between my legs, rubbing me through my panties, I knew the answer was yes, yes, I was. I closed my eyes and focused on the sensation of his big, rough hand on my most sensitive spot, pleasure pulsing out of me, Jack knowing just where I wanted his touch.

"That feel good, gorgeous?" he asked. His voice was low, heavy with arousal.

"So damn good. Don't stop."

He didn't. Instead, Jack pulled my panties to the side and continued to touch me, his bare skin against mine. I moaned, already feeling the stirrings of an orgasm. The man was an expert, finding my clit and making slow circles around it, each motion bringing me to another level of delight.

Jack touched me and teased me and built just the right amount of anticipation before spreading my lips and entering me with a finger. I was beyond wet by that point, his digit pushing into me with ease, my walls gripping him. I let out a cry, bucking in his hand. His finger felt so good, so damn good, but it being inside of me only made me crave his cock more.

He held fast over top of me, gazing down as he worked with his hand. The orgasm built and built until I was right on the brink.

"Come for me," he said. "Right now."

There was something about his stern, insistent voice that I couldn't resist. I did as he instructed, releasing and letting the climax rip through my body. I pressed my face against his arm next to me, soft whimpers of total pleasure filling the air.

The orgasm crested and receded. When it was gone, all I wanted was more.

I opened my eyes and reached down, undoing his belt, button and zipper with an intensity that was practically frantic. Jack chuckled as he helped.

"Easy, little lady. We've got all night, you know."

I couldn't help but smile at his words and easy tone. Gruff and even standoffish as he might've been, there was something to Jack that was also comfortable and calming, something that made me feel safe despite him being two shades away from being a total stranger.

"We do. But that doesn't mean I can wait even another second."

He chuckled again as he did the rest of the work of opening his jeans. I grabbed onto them and his boxer briefs, yanking both down. His cock sprang out, his length and thickness so much that my eyes went wide at the sight of it.

How the hell...

I pushed aside my concerns at the logistics of fitting his massive member inside of me, and instead went to it. I wrapped my fingers around him, my hand seeming so small in comparison to what I was holding.

Jack closed his eyes and growled as I began to stroke him, my grip sliding up and down his length, my fingertips teasing the ridge of his head. Part of me wanted to make him come right then and there, to feel his cock pulse in my hands as he drained.

Jack had other ideas in mind. He lowered himself, the tip of his cock grazing my lips and sending another shiver of delight up my spine. He positioned his head right at my entrance. I felt practically electric knowing that he was moments from being inside me.

"Shit," he said, his voice low. "Protection. Lemme go grab something."

Before he could move, however, I placed my hands on his rear and held him in place, making sure he didn't go anywhere.

"Don't worry about it. I'm on the pill."

The corner of his mouth curled. "Good. Because even the two minutes it would take to run to the other room would be pure torture."

"Ditto."

He replaced his cock where it had been moments before, this time pushing into me. His head entered, tingling spreading through my entire body as if his dick were freaking magic. Jack moved in slowly, inch by inch. I could sense that he was well aware of how big he was and knew it might be a lot for a woman to handle.

The sensation of him pushing into me was beyond intense. I kept my eyes open, watching as his thick cock vanished inside of me, disappearing between my legs. The feeling of him moving inside was unlike anything I'd ever felt, his thickness stretching me as the wetness of my arousal helped him to glide right in.

"Wow," I moaned.

He grinned as he pushed the rest of the way inside, filling me completely.

"I take it that feels good."

"Y-yeah." The sensation of him completely inside of me was so intense that I couldn't say a single word other than that.

Jack reached up, peeling off my sports bra, my breasts tumbling out. He leaned down and took one into his hands, his mouth wrapping around my nipple and his tongue lashing it, making it hard. I arched my back, his cock unmoving inside of me as he gave my breasts attention.

When he was good and ready, he lifted his hips and withdrew, pushing into me hard. I took him much more easily and Jack repeated his thrust again and again, pleasure building inside of me.

I wrapped my legs around his hips and my arms around his back, my hands falling onto his powerful muscles. I focused on the broad muscles of his back tensing underneath my touch and each time he entered in and out of me, his grunts sounding next to my ear as he thrust into me at a steady, pulsing pace that put me into a trance.

"More," I moaned. "Please. Harder."

The words coming out of my mouth sounded distant, as if the ecstasy of him inside of me were an out-of-body experience. Another orgasm began to build, and I could sense that Jack was drawing close to one of his own.

I wanted to see it happen. I wanted to feel his entire body tense as he erupted; I wanted to feel his cock shoot deep inside me.

"Come for me," I said. "Please."

He opened his brilliant blue eyes.

"You first."

With that, he rose onto his knees, grabbing my ankles and lifting my legs, holding them up on either shoulder as he crashed into me again and again. The position gave me a full view of his incredible body, and in that moment all I could think about was that he was some sort of machine built for pleasuring me and me alone.

I couldn't resist any longer. I came, my back arching once more as an impossibly intense orgasm broke. My legs shook in his hands, my body thrashing and writhing as I was pushed over the edge. Jack came too, letting out one more hard grunt as he allowed himself to go over the point of no return, his cock throbbing inside of me.

He held our position, his pace slowing until finally he stopped, his powerful, broad chest expanding and contracting as he regained his breath. I held out my arms for him, and Jack fell down next to me.

I rolled over, Jack wrapping an arm around me as we watched the flames together. The events of the day began to settle in my mind, a strange, sudden fatigue taking hold. The last thoughts I had before drifting off, my eyes on the fire, were how oddly happy I was laying there naked with a man I barely knew.

~

I opened my eyes, realizing right away that I was someplace I hadn't been before. I was in a bedroom, a small, but cozy space that looked out onto the back stretch of property behind the cabin. Sunlight poured in, and I felt more rested and refreshed than I had in a long time. A warm feeling instantly ran through me as I realized that Jack had carried me off the couch and brought me into his spare room.

My parents! They must be worried sick about me. Although I was able to have a brief exchange with Mom the day before using Jack's phone, I realized I never responded to her last text—she had no details, no definitive location of where I was or who I was with. Knowing my parents it would be no surprise to see them in the big plow truck eventually pulling into Jack's driveway after driving all around Wheeler Hill and the surrounding areas. I knew I had to get a message to them as quickly as I could.

I rolled out of bed, placing my feet on the floor, the

round rug beneath warm and toasty against my skin. Once I was up, I stepped over to the window and looked out, the forest around the cabin glistening with fresh, shimmering snow, the sky above clear and blue. I was in a T-shirt that went all the way down to my knees, and a quick check of the room revealed that my clothes had been neatly folded and placed on a chair in the corner.

I'd slept with a strange man who I'd barely known for a few hours. That had *never* happened before in my life. I could count the number of men I'd been with on one hand, and not a single one of them had I slept with before we'd been on more than a few dates.

Jack was *different*. Something about him had made me want to give myself over, to put myself into his hands as if I were his. It was weird, and way too much to think about.

I reached down and grabbed hold of the T-shirt, taking in the scent of it. It smelled like Jack, musky and sensual. Part of me wanted to keep it.

Shit. What the hell am I going to say to him? It's going to be so awkward when I go out there.

Didn't matter, it had to be done. I quickly threw on my clothes and stepped out of the bedroom after making the bed. I entered a long hallway. The longer I stood there, the more I began to realize that I'd vastly misjudged the size of the place. A few doors were along the hall, and at the far end was a flight of stairs that went up to a second floor. Between the dark and the ding I'd given my head, clearly I'd missed how large the cabin actually was.

I slowly made my way down the hall, listening for any sign that Jack was up and about.

I heard nothing other than the soft crackling of a fire. After making my way down the hall, I entered the living room. It was neat and tidy, the mess from our fun the night before gone. The small fire kept the space toasty, Buddy curled up in front of it. He lifted his head as I entered, getting up and coming over to me.

"Hey, Bud," I said, scratching the top of his head. Buddy was powerful-looking and handsome, the perfect companion for the man who owned him.

As I gave Buddy some pets, I looked around the place. The kitchen was to the left, the space big and open, the dishes we'd set out to dry already put away. A bit of coffee was in the carafe, the sight of it inviting me to pour myself a cup and sip it in front of the fire.

There were a few pairs of boots near the front door, a couple of coats hung on a hook beside it. The place was still and quiet.

Part of me wanted to look around for him, at least to tell him thanks for what he'd done. Another part, the bigger part, knew I had to get the hell out of there. Would I be able to resist running into his arms and letting him take me over and over?

I knew I needed to contact Mom to let her know I was OK. I would need to borrow Jack's phone again to do that. I let out a sigh, knowing that I was going to have to find Jack as quickly as possible. I gave Buddy one more pet before heading outside. As I began toward the door, however, I spotted Jack's phone on the end table. I picked it up and shot off a quick text message to Mom, letting her know that I was OK and asking if they could come and pick me up. She answered immediately with an enthusiastic yes! and asked me to send her a pin of my location.

Fifteen minutes later I spotted my parents' big plow truck entering the long driveway. I gave Buddy one last scratch and tried to ignore the sad look on his face. I stepped outside into the bright, sunny day, the sparkling snow infusing with the sunlight making me wish I had a pair of shades. I waved as I walked toward the truck, Mom and Dad excitedly returning the gesture.

I stepped up into the big truck and took a deep breath as I looked back at the cabin, Buddy in the window watching as we pulled away. While I wasn't sure I'd ever see Jack again, there was no doubt that I'd never forget the night we shared.

CHAPTER 6

JACK

"Goddamn, you taste good."

A groan slipped out of me as I watched Beth work. She was between my knees, wearing nothing but a skimpy set of black bra and panties, a smile on her face as she licked my cock up and down.

"Talk is cheap, gorgeous," I said. "*Show* me how much you like the taste of it."

I watched as she opened her mouth, wrapping her lips around my head and forming a tight seal. While I couldn't see her tongue, I sure as hell could feel it flick against me. I reached down, sweeping her hair away from her face—I wanted to see every detail of what she was doing.

Beth sucked and licked, opening her mouth for long enough to kiss up and down my length before returning to the top and taking me inside again. Soft, wet sounds filled the air, and I could feel the orgasm building.

"You know what I want," she said, her voice heavy and sultry.

"You're going to have to earn it."

She made a faux sad face as she continued to stroke me. "What, you don't think I am?"

"You most definitely are. But don't you dare stop."

Beth grinned. "I won't. And in return, you've got to give me every last drop."

"Deal."

She returned to her work, bringing her tongue down my length and looking up at me with those shimmering eyes. The sight of Beth on her knees with a mouthful of me was about the sexiest goddamn thing I could imagine. And the more she sucked, the closer I came.

The sharp sound of a dog barking snapped me out of my fantasy. I rolled over in bed, draping my arm over where someone else would be if I were sleeping next to them. My arm fell onto nothing, of course—no one had shared my bed in years. Well, other than Buddy when I was in the mood to let him sleep at the foot.

I sat up, wiping the sleep from my eyes. Buddy was still barking, which was strange. A well-trained hound like him knew better than to bark obnoxiously like some rich lady's purse puppy. I knew that something was up.

"Easy, Bud!" I called out. "You're gonna wake up our guest!"

I checked my watch, seeing that it was a little after eight. It was later than I normally liked to sleep in, but after the night I'd had, I figured I'd earned it.

I was in nothing but boxer briefs, my usual sleepwear. As I made my way around the foot of the bed, I took a quick glance at myself in the mirror. My body still looked fine and strong, but the cold weather had made me slack when it came to working out. Sure, I had a home gym, but there was something about freezing temps that made me have a hard time hitting the iron. As I threw on some jeans and a gray T-shirt, I made a mental note to get in a good, long lift when I came back from dropping Beth off back home.

I stepped into the hallway. Right away I noticed that the door to the guest room was open. I headed over and peeked inside.

She was gone. The bed was made and her clothes were absent from the chair. I shut the door and headed into the living room, half expecting to find her there.

But there was no sign of her. Buddy was at the window, looking out and barking.

"What's the story, Bud?" I asked, stepping over to the window and patting his haunches. "There a reason you're barking like a damn madman?"

The moment I looked out of the window, however, I realized right away what he was so damn upset about. Tire tracks cut through the snow on the drive in front of the house—fresh ones, by the look of it.

"Come on. Let's go check it out."

I threw on a coat and stepped into my boots before opening the front door, a blast of frigid air greeting me. The weather was decent, nice and sunny with some fine-looking powder. I needed to run into town for a few supplies, so it pleased me to see the weather appeared to be accommodating. I'd still need to hitch the plow onto the front of the truck, but that'd take no time at all.

I headed over to the end of my front yard. Right away it was clear that someone had arrived in a big truck, maybe one similar to mine.

"Well, Bud," I said, putting my hands on my hips. "Doesn't take a genius to figure out that she flew the coop."

Buddy came over, sitting down next to me and looking over the scene as if double-checking my findings.

She was gone. I wasn't hurt or offended, of course; I

knew she most definitely wanted to get back home, and there was no doubt her parents were worried sick about her.

All the same, I already missed the girl, as strange as it was to admit. Part of me had hoped that we might spend the morning together—have a little breakfast, maybe even have some more of the fun we'd had last night.

I let out a sigh, shaking my head as I turned back toward the cabin. Part of me felt a touch foolish that I was experiencing such sentiments over a woman I barely knew. Another part was more definitive, feeling like someone special had come into my life and now she was gone.

You're forgetting one detail, pal—she was half your damn age.

I was still having trouble wrapping my head around that one. I'd had a few flings here and there over the years since Charlotte, my late wife, had passed. They'd all been closer to my age and not one of them had made the impression on me that Beth had.

She was beautiful and brilliant and full of life. I wanted to know more about the plans she'd hinted at, the life she lived back in civilization. It was odd for me to have that thought, yet there it was.

As I trudged through the snow back to the cabin, it occurred to me that Beth might very well be dangerous to the barrier I'd built around my heart. I might not have been happy about the way she'd left, but maybe it was for the best that she did.

I opened the cabin door and stepped inside, Buddy following in close behind. I pulled off my coat and tossed it onto the rack before grabbing some fresh wood and bringing it over to the fireplace. I set it into the flames and watched it crackle, my mind once more drifting to Beth.

I guessed she was somewhere in her mid-twenties. That

was about the same age Charlotte was when she'd passed. Beth had reminded me of her in more ways than one. They were both sharp, smart, and weren't afraid to tell you just what they thought of anything.

My mind drifted further as I gazed into the fire, watching the orange flames wrap around the fresh log. I found myself thinking about the day I'd lost Charlotte, that knock at my front door that'd changed my life forever.

The ring of my phone cut through the air, snapping me out of my daydream.

"Alright, alright."

I put my hands on my knees and pushed myself up, stretching as I stepped over to where my phone lay on the table next to the front door. I checked the screen and saw that it was a call from Beau, my twenty-five-year-old son, the only child from my marriage to Charlotte.

I flicked the phone open and held it to my ear.

"Beau!" I said, a small smile forming on my lips. "What's the word?"

"Dad? You there? I can barely hear you."

His voice was crackling and cutting out.

"Hold on a sec, let me go to the guest bedroom."

Beau replied with a word I could barely hear before I started down the hall to the bedroom. The guest room was one of the only places in the house with halfway decent reception.

"Dad?" Beau's voice became clearer the closer I moved to the bedroom.

"Yo, kiddo," I said as I stepped over the threshold of the room.

"OK, there we go," Beau replied. "Hey Dad, you know they make these things called smart phones, right? They're awesome—you can see people's faces on the screen, and they tend to get better reception than phones that are almost as old as I am."

"They're also made of glass, kid," I said. "Drop the end of a hatchet on the front of that phone of yours and tell me how nice the screen looks."

He laughed. "Yeah, yeah. I know better by this point than to try to change your mind about anything, let alone your phone."

I dropped into the chair in the corner of the room, the one where I'd placed Beth's clothes. I gazed out the window, the fresh, white snow almost as bright as the sky above. Part of me wanted to get out there, maybe go for a walk with Buddy.

"Anyway, what's up?" I asked, propping my feet on the small writing desk next to me.

A pause followed that was long enough to catch my attention.

"What're you doing tonight?" he asked finally.

"Nothing. Got to run into town, but other than that I was planning on having a—"

"Let me guess," he said, interrupting me. "A quiet night in."

"Something wrong with that?" I almost told him that I'd earned it after the sort of night I'd had prior. I caught myself, however, not wanting to mention that I'd spent the previous night sleeping with a woman far closer to his age than mine.

"I mean, no. But when every single night of yours is a quiet night in, it kind of starts to raise the question of if that life of yours up there in the woods is doing you any favors."

I let out a sarcastic laugh. "Is my own son telling me how to live my life? Again?"

"No. You do you, Dad. Just saying that sometimes I wish you lived closer."

"A thirty-minute drive isn't close enough for you?"

"It's about more than the time it takes to drive to your place. You're just so isolated up there."

"I'm not alone, I've got Buddy. And it's not like I'm here puttering around in my cabin all day. I've got my work, and I've got plenty of shit to do around the property." I took my feet off the desk, sitting up. "And what the hell am I doing explaining myself to my own damn kid?"

"Alright, Dad, easy. I didn't call to give you the third degree about how you spend your time."

"Starting to feel that way."

"Well, I'm sorry. The reason I called is that I wanted to see if you felt like doing dinner over here with Megan and me."

"Dinner at your place? What's the occasion?"

He chuckled. "Does there have to be an occasion? Can't a son want to spend time with his own dad?"

"I suppose so. But you have to admit that it's not often you're inviting me over to your place. It's enough to make a man wonder if there's something more going on than just dinner."

"Maybe there is." He left it at that.

"Well, you going to tell me? You know I hate surprises."

"And Megan loves them."

"Tell him it'll be fun!" the voice of Megan, Beau's girlfriend, sounded in the background. "And Buddy can come too!"

"You heard it, Dad," Beau said. "It'll be fun. Come on. We're doing the cooking. All you have to do is show up. Then again, I wouldn't complain if you brought a bottle of good whiskey over."

There wasn't much to think about.

"What time?"

"Come around six. We'll have drinks while Megan and I finish cooking."

"That's doable. I'll see you then, kid."

"Looking forward to it."

The call ended and Buddy came into the room, sitting down on the floor in front of me.

"Well, Bud, looks like we're heading into town tonight."

He whimpered, letting me know it was time for a walk.

"Alright, alright." I put my hands on my knees and prepared to stand. As I did, I spotted something black underneath the end of the bed. I rose from my seat and went over, snatching it from the ground and holding it up in front of me.

It was the black panties that Beth had been wearing last night. I let out a snort of a laugh, tossing them onto the bed.

"Come on, Bud."

Buddy and I headed out of the room but the damage had been done—the sight of the panties had put Beth back into my head, and once she was there I didn't want to let her out. Between her, and whatever the hell was going on with Beau, it seemed my life had suddenly become full of surprises.

CHAPTER 7

JACK

Snow crunched under my boots as I trudged from my car to the condo where my son Beau and his girlfriend Megan lived. It was a nice enough place, one of those newer buildings that were like big squares with steel bottoms and accent walls of orange and blue. I carried a bottle of good whiskey in one hand, a neatly wrapped package of venison in the other.

All the same, I felt strange whenever I came into town and had to be around people. Beau and Megan didn't exactly live in the beating heart of Denver, but when you lived out in the woods like I did, even a suburb had a way of feeling like a megalopolis. Still, I loved having my son close.

I stepped up to the front door of the condo and prepared to knock.

"Don't need to do that, Dad. Remember?"

Beau's voice came from the small TV screen to the left of the door. Beau's face was there, and I remembered that he had one of those fancy-ass security systems you could access from an app.

"Right. Well, I'm here."

"I can see that. Be down in a sec."

The screen went black. A moment later I heard the thud-thud of someone approaching, then the door opened and there he was.

"Dad!" Beau exclaimed. "Good to see you."

My son Beau was twenty-five-years-old, tall and strapping with a handsome face and head of dark hair. It was always damn surreal to look at the kid—though he was hardly a kid anymore. He had my features, my powerful jaw and deep-set eyes. But he was clean-shaven, his clothes neat, the boots he wore more for fashion than utility. He was me if I lived in town and worked in tech rather than living on a mountain.

His eyes were the same deep, forest green with flecks of gold as his mother's. It was hard not to feel the bite of her loss all over again when I looked into them.

"Likewise, kiddo."

We gave one another a big hug, Beau giving me a slap on my back, nearly knocking the bottle of whiskey from my hand.

"Easy, big man," I said with a slight chuckle. "Unless you want to be cleaning this fine whiskey off the floor."

He stepped back, flashing me a smile and glancing down at the goods in my hands.

"Well, what've we got here?"

"Hello, Jack."

Stepping around the corner was Megan Goodjohn, Beau's girlfriend of a couple years. I was on the fence about Megan. She was smart and successful—already high in the ranks of one Denver non-profit or another, her attitude and the way she carried herself a reflection of the reasons for her success. She was polished and pretty and well put together; the type of woman who had her life planned out to the minute in her day planner with different colored highlighters.

It was no secret that she wasn't too crazy about my lifestyle. Made no difference to me—I'd never been the kind of man to wait around for permission to do anything. But it did result in a bit of tension now and then.

"Megan," I said. "Always a pleasure."

She flashed me one of her usual prim smiles, the kind where you couldn't tell if she was being polite or snooty.

"What have we got there?" she asked, coming over to me for a quick hug.

"Whiskey and venison. You ask me, not a finer combination on earth."

She took the package and looked it over, as if there was something hidden and secret about it. "Did you kill and dress this one yourself?"

Megan was the type who was more than a little squeamish about where food came from, and she'd never been big on meat. No doubt she was imagining me standing in front of a deer carcass with a big knife in my hand, blood and guts everywhere.

"Only way to do it," I said. "Right from the source."

"Well, I'm doing a vegan diet for the time being but I'm sure Beau will enjoy it." She passed the package back to me. "Anyway, come on into the kitchen, we've got guests." She flicked her eyes down to my feet. "And... if you wouldn't mind leaving those boots here at the entrance, that'd be most appreciated."

Without another word, she turned and headed out of the room.

"Real charmer," I said with a smile, keeping my voice low.

"Be nice," Beau said right back.

He took the whiskey and venison and I clapped my hand on his shoulder. Megan and I weren't exactly cut from the same cloth, but we had one important thing in common, maybe *the* most important thing—we were both crazy about Beau. Nothing else mattered.

Beau and I headed out of the entry hall and toward the kitchen, the sounds of conversation drifting in our direction. My gut tightened. I wasn't shy but I didn't care much for rubbing elbows. Truth of the matter was, I'd been looking forward to a quiet night with my boy.

We entered the kitchen and I was greeted with the smell of something cooking in the oven and the sight of an older couple, both exquisitely dressed and poised. They instantly reminded me of Megan—the way they looked and carried themselves were very similar.

"Well, if it isn't the man we've all been waiting for!"

The man was tall and thin with a head of thinning hair and gold-rimmed glasses. He approached for a handshake and I gave him one, though I found it a little weak and insincere.

"Martin Goodjohn," he said. "Real pleasure to finally get to meet you."

"Jackson Oliver. But most people just call me Jack."

The woman offered her hand next. I was far from an expert on such matters, but one look at her hand and nails gave me the distinct impression that she spent more on manicures in a month than I spent on Buddy's dog chow, and I fed him the good stuff.

"Celina Goodjohn," she said. "Very nice to meet you."

She flicked her eyes down at *my* hand, as if expecting to find grease under my fingernails. All the same, we shook.

"Well," I said, looking around. "We've got ourselves a bit of a gathering here, looks like."

"That's right, Jack," Megan said. "That's because tonight is a special night."

Beau spoke next. "Megan and I have been talking and decided that too much damn time has gone by without you all meeting."

"Not easy to have get-togethers like this when you're living in New York," Martin said.

"Or in the middle of the woods," Megan added.

"And while our lives are quite chaotic these days," Celina began, "We figured, oh, why not? Nothing like a bit of mountain air to boost one's vitality, right? I mean, you would know, living the life that you do."

While Megan intentionally made her little digs about my lifestyle, I got the sense that it wasn't like that with her parents. They simply appeared to be a wealthy couple from New York who couldn't imagine living in the woods and weren't quite sure how to talk about the subject. I'd never been one to be easily offended, and I wasn't about to start then.

"Hell, it's a big part of the reason why I do it. When you spend as much time as I do out in nature you can almost taste the dirt in the air when you come back into town."

"Dirt in the air," Megan said. "Charming description. Anyway, dinner's about ready. Shall we sit and get started?"

With that, we gathered around the table and took our places.

"Sure smells good, whatever it is," I said, pulling out my chair and easing into it.

"Vegan pot roast," Megan said with a proud smile.

"Vegan pot roast?" I asked. "What's the *roast* part?"

"Mushrooms and potatoes," Beau answered. "It's... good."

I had to stifle a laugh. Beau was an easygoing guy, the

type of man who'd have no problem accommodating something like Megan's fad-diet-hopping. Me, I couldn't imagine a meal without meat.

"Guess we're not going to be using the venison," I replied. "In that case, I'm going double on the whiskey." I reached for the bottle and pulled off the cap. "You all want a bit?"

"I'm more of a Cabernet kind of guy," Martin replied. "But why not?"

"Just a tiny bit for me," Celina added.

"I'll take more than a tiny bit," Beau said.

I poured the drinks and got the distinct impression that there was something heavy on Beau's mind, something he was a touch nervous about. It was unlike him. He was a city boy, but he'd always had the same spine and fearlessness that I did.

We toasted and drank, the whiskey hitting me just right.

"So," Martin said. "Beau tells us that you're in the accounting game."

"That's right. Mostly out of it now, freelancing stuff here and there."

"Who did you work for?" asked Celina. "If you don't mind us prying."

"The world of business is smaller than you may think," Martin added. "You and I might know the same people. Always fun to find out such things."

I tensed. The subject of my past, the sort of men I worked for... that wasn't up for dinnertime discussion. Beau glanced at me out of the corner of his eye, likely wondering just how I was going to handle the situation.

"Not likely," I said. "Never worked for large companies or anything like that. Always plied my trade with private types—independently wealthy folks who wanted a careful eye looking over their books."

It was my go-to story. There was no way in hell the truth of my clientele would ever be discussed in mixed, unfamiliar company, especially not after all the trouble I'd gone to in order to leave it behind.

"That's a fine way to do it," Martin said. "Wading into the business world certainly has its perks. But independent contracting has its own set of benefits as well."

"Anyway," Celina added. "We're in town to get away from work, not to discuss it." She glanced in her daughter's direction. "Not to mention the little surprise you both have in store for us."

I sat back, holding my drink near my middle. "Yeah, what's this surprise, kid?"

Beau and Megan shared one of those glances couples gave one another when they'd reached the point in their relationship where they didn't need words to communicate. I could sense they were trying to figure out the best way to go about telling us.

"Why not?" Beau finally asked. "Let's share the good news now."

"We wanted to wait until after dinner," Megan added. "But I suppose there's no reason why we can't share it beforehand."

They took one another's hands; I took a sip of my whiskey.

Beau started. "As you all know, Megan and I have been together for quite some time now."

"Two years, eight months, and eleven days," she said, smiling good-naturedly at him. "Not like I'm keeping track."

Beau smiled warmly back at her, patting her hand. "Can't even remember what it was like before we were together, you know? Guess that's how love makes you feel, like life before it was a little less meaningful. So, that's why we're finally taking the next step, we're—"

"We're getting married!" Megan exclaimed the words, her eyes lighting up with total happiness as she spoke.

"Oh, my goodness!" Martin said. "That's wonderful!"

Megan let out a scream of excitement, her mother doing the same. Beau shrugged, and I got the sense that he'd had a whole speech planned that had just been cutoff halfway through.

"Married?" I asked. "Kiddo, that's amazing!" I reached over and patted his shoulder.

"When is this happening?" Celina asked. "Summer, I'm guessing?"

Megan shook her head. "Nope. When Beau proposed we decided that we didn't want to waste a second making it happen. We called the venue we wanted and told them that we would like to make a reservation for the soonest day possible."

Celina cocked her head to the side, a tinge of apprehension on her face. "And... when was that?"

"May sixth!" Megan exclaimed.

Celina had been thrilled moments ago. This revelation, however, took the smile right off her face.

"You're not serious, are you?" she asked. "Megan, it's January! The middle of January at that! You honestly think that we can plan a wedding in that short of an amount of time? Your father and I had nine months to plan ours, and *that* was rushing it!"

"Mom, it's going to be fine. We've already done some research, and..."

Celina interrupted her, the two of them descending into

a back-and-forth about the logistics of the upcoming wedding.

"Congrats, son," I said, raising my glass.

"Thanks, Dad." He raised his, too.

Martin slipped his phone out of his pocket, his eyes flashing as he took in whatever was on the screen.

"Shoot, I need to take this. Congrats!" He sprang out of his seat and was gone.

Dinner came and went, most of it occupied by Megan and her mother going back and forth over wedding details. Martin returned to the table only to get right back up out of his chair when another call came in. I poked at my "pot roast," which didn't taste all that bad, really. It also didn't even come close to filling me up.

Toward the end of dinner, Martin on another call, Megan having busted out her laptop right at the table to research some wedding stuff with her mother, I nodded to Beau, gesturing for him to come outside with me. He smiled and nodded, grabbing the bottle of whiskey.

A few moments later we were out on the balcony, the space heater going and the lights of Denver visible off in the distance. Beau opened the bottle of whiskey and poured me a stiff measure.

"Thank you kindly, son," I said. "Don't want to speak out of turn here, but if I had to listen to another minute of that bickering…"

"I know, I know. You were good in there. People like her parents aren't exactly your preferred company, and I appreciate you making the effort."

"They were fine," I said. "Standard rich folks." I stopped myself before saying more, not wanting to speak out of turn.

Beau smiled, seeming to understand what I'd been about to say but not upset about the subject matter.

"Go on, spit it out."

I sighed, shaking my head and taking another sip of my drink. I had a good buzz going by that point and while I'd never had a problem speaking my mind ever in my life, the whiskey had me even more eager than I normally would be.

"You're sure about Megan?"

He nodded, his smile fading as he turned his gaze back to the city off in the distance. I had the immediate impression that I'd asked something he'd anticipated me asking him but hoped I wouldn't.

"Yeah, I know you don't like her."

"Now, that's not it at all."

"Is that right? Because if a parent's not happy about their kid marrying someone, it's a pretty solid assumption that he doesn't like them."

"It's not a matter of *liking* her. She's a nice enough woman, comes from a good family, well educated, all the important stuff. It's just... she's a little high-strung, you know? Men in our family, we're independent down to the last. A woman like Megan, she's gonna be plotting out your days down to the second, dragging you from trips to charity events to dinners and all that shit. Can't imagine a guy like you being happy in a relationship like that."

"I get what you're saying. But the way I look at it is, well, we balance each other out, you know? She's got her work and her schedule and her day planner, and my job's the total opposite. I can work whenever, wherever. I'm easygoing, fine with whatever, and that rubs off on her, too."

His expression turned tense, letting me know he had something else on his mind.

"There's... something else, too."

"What is it?"

"As I've already told you, Megan's moving up in her company. And a few weeks ago, well, she got an offer."

"What kind of offer?"

"One that would take her to New York."

And there it was. I sighed, shaking my head as I looked out onto the city. His words hit me like a punch in the gut, and I wasn't quite sure how I felt.

"That's part of the reason we wanted to rush the wedding a little. Megan was dead set on us being married before we moved, said she wanted us to start our new journey together as an actual married couple."

"Cute."

"Not to mention that she said it wouldn't look professional to be an unmarried couple shacking up. We'll make our big arrival to the city as Mr. and Mrs. Oliver. Well, Goodjohn-Oliver in her case."

"Aw, hell, she's going with the hyphen thing?"

"*Dad.*"

"I know, I know, times are changing. Don't forget that I'm an old man."

"I don't," he said with a small grin.

I turned my attention back to the horizon, sipping my drink and not saying a word. Too much was on my mind to try and speak.

"What're you thinking, Dad? I know this is a hell of a lot to take in."

"Not thinking about anything. Well actually I'm thinking about the venison I'm gonna be cooking up when I get home. Vegan pot roast. I swear to God, Beau."

"You know what I mean. You never like to talk about what's on your mind or in your heart, and that's fine, I get it.

But I want to hear you at least say you're happy, even if you aren't."

"Of course, I'm happy. My boy's getting married to a woman he loves. How the hell else could I feel? Sure, I have my misgivings about Megan, but at the end of the day you love one another, and that's all that matters. I guess… I guess I'm just thinking about how much I'm gonna hate it when my boy's no longer a thirty-minute drive away. I like having you here, Beau. And I don't know if you two have talked about having kids, but damned if I haven't dreamt about grandkids—my son bringing his little tykes over to the cabin and showing them how their granddaddy lives."

He pursed his lips and nodded. "I get it. This isn't going to be easy. And I know you don't want to hear it, but I'm not crazy about the idea of you living by yourself in that cabin."

"I'm fine out there."

"You're fine for *now*. But don't act like you're going to be coming into civilization as much as you do with me being here. Last thing I want is to come visit and see you with a giant gray beard and a wild look in your eyes talking to squirrels or some such nonsense."

"This beard ain't gray just yet. And why the hell would I talk to squirrels? I've got Buddy."

He laughed for a moment, another pensive expression taking hold.

"Dad, have you ever thought about, you know… finding someone?"

"No."

"Yeah, that's what you always say."

"You honestly want me to disrespect your mother's memory by finding someone else?"

"It's not disrespecting Mom's memory. You deserve to have someone, Dad. And do you really think Mom would be happy that you're planning on spending the rest of your life alone out in the woods?" He pressed his lips into a thin line, and I could tell that something else was on his mind.

"Go for it," I said. "Spit it out, tell me what you've got knocking around up there."

"Fine. You know what I think? I think that *you* think you don't deserve anyone. I think you feel like you did things you shouldn't have when I was little, and because of that you believe you deserve to be alone until you die. No matter how much you've changed."

I said nothing, slowly sipping my whiskey. Did the kid have a point? Maybe. But I wasn't about to argue with him knowing I only had a short time before he was gone halfway across the country.

"I'll think about it." Not a chance in hell I would be doing that, but it was my way of ending the argument.

"Good. I just want you to be happy, Dad. Maybe it's because of the way I feel about Megan, but damn if it wouldn't go a long way knowing you had someone, too."

Silence fell, another one of my ways to let the subject pass.

"I'm gonna miss you, kid. I'm proud as hell of you, and I'm thrilled you're about to get hitched. Don't let my cranky-ass nature make you think I feel anything but total happiness for you. Got it?"

He smiled. "Got it. I should get back in there. You coming?"

"Yeah, after I finish my drink I'll head in."

He nodded, pushing off the balcony to step inside.

"And Beau?"

"Yeah?"

"I love you. I know I don't say it enough, but all the same I don't ever want you to doubt it."

"I love you too, Dad."

With that, he went back inside. I sipped my drink, alone with my thoughts and the endless city sprawled out before me.

Part of me worried he was right; maybe I was on the verge of spending my life puttering around in my cabin alone until I finally croaked. What if it didn't have to be that way? As soon as the thought occurred to me, Beth appeared in my mind.

I had no business thinking about a young woman I'd had a one-off with. All the same, I couldn't shake her from my thoughts. And it scared the hell out of me.

CHAPTER 8

BETH

Two months later…

"No way. No *freaking* way."

Janie Hoffman, my best friend since high school and now roommate, had a huge grin on her face.

"Yes way. Yes *freaking* way."

I wanted to say something in response, to at least shoot her a hard look. But all I could do was stare at the pregnancy test in front of me.

Positive. It was *positive*. Granted, it was the same result I'd had with the two others that I'd taken but there was something about *this* test that really made it sink in.

I was pregnant.

I blinked hard, dropping back onto the couch and resumed staring off into space.

"You OK over there?"

Janie, petite and curly-haired with big dark eyes and a full mouth that always seemed to be smiling, waved her hand in front of me.

"Uh, you there, B?"

It took me a moment to attempt a response. The world felt like an old war movie I'd seen my dad watching when I was a kid, where the battle scene was slowed down with spacey audio to give it a surreal vibe.

Surreal. That's how it all felt. The idea that there was a tiny person inside of me growing bigger and bigger with each passing moment... I didn't even know where to begin to wrap my head around it.

"Yeah, I'm here."

"Let me get you some water. Hold on."

She zipped out of my field of vision, hurrying over to the adjoining kitchen. Our Denver condo wasn't huge or all that impressive, but it was home. Most importantly, it was my first real adult place outside of the dorms and low-rent apartments where I'd lived during college.

Janie returned, pushing the glass of water into my hand.

"Sip. Take a drink. You just got the shock of a lifetime, lady."

"Thanks," I said, taking a sip of water.

"You ok?" Janie asked.

"I can't believe what I'm looking at." I lifted my eyes from the pregnancy test and brought them to my best friend. "How the hell is this even possible?"

"Well, when a man and a woman love each other very much..."

That got a laugh out of me. "OK, shush. There was no love involved when this happened." I sighed. "But what I mean is how could this happen when I was on the freaking pill?"

Janie pursed her lips, giving the matter some thought. "Well, the pill's only ninety-nine percent effective."

"So that means I hit the one-out-of-a-hundred screw

that got me knocked up."

"Not necessarily. The pill technically has a near-perfect effectiveness rate. The one percent part takes into consideration, well, uh... user error."

"Like, I screwed up taking it?"

"More or less. Now, I don't exactly know how it happened, but I *do* know that you've been insanely busy with your business, the move, and a lot of stuff over the last few months. If I had to guess, I'd say that you, well, weren't one hundred percent on top of things when it came to taking your pills on time."

I opened my mouth and raised my finger, ready to tell her that she was talking out of her butt, that I was great about those kinds of things. The more I thought about it, however, the more I began to realize that she was probably right—that I'd gotten so wrapped up with everything crazy in my life that I'd slipped up.

I lowered my finger and sat back, letting out a sigh.

"I guess when you're not having sex it doesn't matter if you slip up and forget the pill every now and then," I said. "I still can't believe I got pregnant from having it just one time."

"But you did. With, uh, your mountain-dwelling friend."

I laughed in spite of the worry running through me. "Don't say it like that, you make it sound like he's some weirdo living inside a cave like a troll or something."

"OK, your friend who lives alone in a cabin in the middle of the woods."

I still couldn't believe what had happened with Jack and that two months later I was still thinking about him. I'd lost track of how many times he'd appeared in my dreams, his powerful body and perfect cock on full display.

"Yeah. He's the only guy I've slept with in quite a while. It's definitely his."

"Alright, good. Then it's a matter of tracking him down, right?"

"Nope. Dad insisted on switching us all over to Apple when I had to replace my broken phone. I doubt Mom still has the pin I dropped her the day they came and picked me up. All I know is that he's somewhere in the woods that I can see from the top of Wheeler Hill."

I let out a noise of total frustration as I fell back onto the couch.

"I can't believe this!"

"Well, believe it babe, because it's happening. How are you feeling about it?" she asked gently.

I thought about it for a moment. "I mean, I guess I'm not totally shocked. I've been having some symptoms for a few weeks now. I think in the back of my mind I knew. And even though I wasn't expecting it, it's a baby. It's *my* baby. I can't be upset about that."

Janie grinned. "Yes! This is going to be so fun. And you'd better get your butt ready for Aunt Janie because I'm going to spoil the hell out of that kid."

I smiled back. "You know I'll be taking you up on that when I need a babysitter."

"Deal."

"It's more that with everything going on at work, I don't have time to think about all of this. Where am I going to fit being pregnant in with getting my wedding planning business up and running? It isn't like I can call in sick—I'm my own boss! And I've got the wedding with Beau and Megan coming up really soon and..." I sighed, suddenly feeling majorly overwhelmed.

Janie nodded, as if understanding where I was coming

from. "I get it. But before you get all twisted into knots about this, let me make you some tea." She sprang from the couch and hurried over to the kitchen once more. Janie was a tea freak, so I could only imagine what she had in mind. "Now, I know you're more of a coffee kind of girl, but unless you're planning on developing a taste for decaf, it's time to get into tea land. Chamomile is perfect for a pregnant lady —nice and calming and no caffeine."

I let her talk, focusing on my breathing and doing my best to chill out. All of a sudden, I had the urge to get up, to move around a little. I could still hear Janie talking from the kitchen, filling the air with words as she so often did when she wasn't sure what else to do. I stepped over to the sliding glass doors to our balcony and looked out onto the courtyard, a little bit of snow dusting the ground.

Megan and Beau. Speaking of insane news, I still couldn't get over how I was planning the wedding for my ex who just happened to be marrying the girl who'd played no small role in trying to make my life a living hell back in high school.

How on Earth did I get tangled up in all of this? My mind drifted back to the first meeting with Megan.

"OK, the main thing is this needs to happen fast. Got it?"

She pushed open the doors of the ski lodge events room, stepping into the big space, her heels clicking on the wood floor. The Crested Butte Lodge was one of the most sought-after wedding venues in the Denver metro area, the interior done in classic winter chalet style with wood everywhere and tall fireplaces in each room, the sort of space where you'd dream about curling up in front of a fire with a mug of cocoa or glass of red wine as the snow fell outside.

Megan entered the room, stopping in the middle and putting her hands on her hips, shaking her head.

"God, what a nightmare."

"Nightmare?" I asked, shutting the doors behind us. "Most people would consider having a wedding here to be a dream come true."

She flashed me an annoyed expression. "Well, when you're putting a wedding together and you find out two weeks before the freaking thing that your wedding planner totally fucked up and booked you at the same time another wedding was set to happen, you'll get what I mean."

Megan sighed, shaking her head in total frustration. "We were supposed to have our wedding at the Skylight—you know, the best venue in the city? This was all we could get." She swept her hand toward the grand space around her. "So corny. I mean a ski lodge in Denver? I can't imagine anything more predictable."

Her expensive jewelry jangled as she moved, looking the place over. Just like back in high school, Megan was dressed to make sure everyone around her knew she came from money.

"It's going to be great," I said. "This place is hardly corny to me."

She shot a hard look in my direction. "Of course you would think that." Megan gave my outfit another once-over, as if sizing it up for how tacky and cheap it was according to her. It was more of the same mean girl shit that she'd subjected me to in high school.

"Not to mention that when I naturally fired the wedding planner for making such a huge mistake, I had to go with someone far less experienced. But didn't it turn out well that the only wedding planner I could find on such short notice was my good friend from high school?"

Something I could never figure out about mean girls was how they were always convinced that you and they were "good friends" despite them seemingly going out of their way at every turn to make your life miserable. Was she really that delusional?

"That's right," I replied, staying as chipper as possible. I needed the money and the spot on my resume. "And besides, a lack of experience doesn't matter—results do. So far, I'm two-for-two with planning some seriously kick-ass weddings. I've no doubt that we'll be able to make this one the same."

She turned back to me, as if annoyed by my cheeriness. Truth be told, I wasn't crazy about the idea of working for Megan. The money was too good to turn down, however. Not to mention that if I were able to pull off an amazing wedding on such a short timeline, I'd have the project to show off to any future clients. Something like this could make my career.

"Well, lucky for you, the other planner already did a good amount of groundwork. I can provide what she managed to get done, and you can take it from there." Megan turned, making her way toward me with slow steps. "But make no mistake, Beth, if you screw this up and embarrass me in front of my friends and family..."

Her glare was hard, but I stood firm, keeping that big, sunny smile right on my face.

"Not a chance. You're going to have the wedding of your dreams."

"Here. Drink up!" Janie shoved a big mug of steaming hot tea in front of my face. "Trust me, this is going to do the trick for calming your ass down."

I jumped a bit, my heart beating fast as I came back into the moment. Janie popped her head into my peripheral vision, raising her eyebrows a bit in concern.

"What's going on over there, girlie?"

I took the mug, wrapping my hands around it as I let out an overwhelmed sigh.

"Nothing. Well, not nothing. Thinking about the situation with Megan and Beau."

She pulled in a slow, sharp draw of air as she nodded in understanding of my situation.

"Yeah. Kind of a mess. Planning the wedding of your ex-boyfriend? Not a job I'd be thrilled about."

"It's not even the Beau part. I mean, that does make it a little awkward."

"A *little* awkward? Don't sell yourself short, B. I mean, you guys have been as intimate with each other as two people can be. Like, weren't you each other's first... everything?"

"Not *everything*. But close enough."

"And then he cheated on you. Total prick move. I wouldn't blame you if you wanted to sabotage the freaking wedding."

"Come on, I'm not vindictive. Besides, why would I get bent out of shape about losing a cheater?"

She smiled. "Easy for you to say now. But I remember all those phone calls when you weren't nearly as put together about it."

"I know, I know. That was a long time ago though. Point I'm trying to make is that I'm not feeling weird about this wedding out of jealousy or anything like that."

"It's because of who he's marrying. I get it. Megan Goodjohn is something else."

"You're telling me." I sighed. "But it'll be worth it. I'll pull this thing off, make a crapload of money, and make my name in the wedding planning business all in one fell swoop."

"There you go, winner's attitude all the way." She

slipped her phone out of her pocket and checked the screen. "Shoot, gotta get moving."

"You're working today?"

"You know it. Barb's kid had a doctor's appointment or something so Doc Graham asked if I could finish her shift. Just a couple hours." A worried expression took hold. "But... I don't know how I feel leaving you alone after you just learned you're freaking pregnant. You want me to tell her I can't make it?"

"No way. You don't need to go back on a promise to your boss so you can sit here and listen to me vent."

"You sure? Because if talking trash about Megan Goodjohn is part of the venting..."

I laughed. "Trust me, we'll be doing plenty of that later."

"Alright, how does this sound—I'll do this quick shift, and on the way back I'll grab some Pad Thai from Tuk-Tuk. My treat."

"Sounds perfect."

With that, Janie bounded out of her seat and gave me a big hug. "You've got this, OK? You're a total badass friend and there's no doubt in my mind that you're going to be a total badass mom."

"Thanks, babe. Love you lots."

"You too."

I sipped my tea, watching the clouds roll in from the distance. I reminded myself that I didn't have time to worry or be nervous. Tomorrow, I was going to meet with Megan *and* Beau. I had to be ready.

Scratch that, I *was* ready. Life was throwing some major challenges my way, but I'd never been scared of a little hard work before. Why start now?

CHAPTER 9

BETH

The drive to The Crested Butte Lodge followed a winding road up through the Rockies, towering peaks on the right and the left, a huge drop-off down to the white-coated valley below.

Though I'd done the drive before, it never failed to make my stomach tight. I alternated between keeping my eyes on the road ahead and glancing down at the gorgeous view, Taylor Swift's *Midnights* blasting on the stereo of my Altima.

I sang loudly along to the music, trying to focus on the road, the view, and the job ahead—anything to distract me from the bombshell that had fallen on my life yesterday, news that I was still having trouble processing.

I was going to be a *mom*. And I was most likely going to be doing it alone. Jack had been pretty adamant about liking his solitude. I can't imagine he'd be chomping at the bit to help me raise a baby after a one-night stand. I had to tell Mom and Dad and make appointments and figure out how I was going to do all of it on my own.

I let out a cry of frustration as I pulled along the

sweeping turn that would take me the rest of the way to the lodge. Everything felt so overwhelming, as if a million things were hitting me all at once.

"You've got this," I said out loud, taking the wheel with both hands and staring forward. "When the hell have you ever backed down from a challenge before?"

By the time I made my way around the last big turn, I was ready for the work ahead. The task that day was to get a lay of the land, to speak with some of the staff, and to get all of the info I could that would form the groundwork of the planning.

Although I'd been there before, I couldn't help but think "wow" as the lodge came into view.

The big turn opened up to the resort, and it was hard not to notice how impressive the place was. The Crested Butte Lodge was five stories tall—a gorgeous Swiss-style chalet of rich wood and warm lighting tucked in among the woods and hills. The valley behind was deep and endless, mountains rising to the east. Also to the east was the ski infrastructure; lifts hitched on wires to carry skiers up all the way to the top.

The place was beautiful, a location where anyone would dream of having a wedding. Planning a huge event there wasn't going to be easy, especially on such a short time frame, but I was determined to make it happen. Didn't matter that the bride was a woman who seemed to take pleasure in making my life miserable. Nevertheless, I was going to give her the best, most magical day of her life.

Beau and I hadn't seen one another since our breakup over five years ago, and things had been left tense between us. While I wasn't crazy about what he'd done to me—cheating on me with some freshman in the bathroom at a freaking house party—I didn't hold a grudge. We were practically kids when it happened, and we hadn't been dating all that long.

My mind was swirling by the time I'd found a place to park. I turned off the engine, then grabbed my bag from the passenger's seat. Cold air rushed into the car as I opened the door, and I pulled up my collar to brace against the chill.

It was so quiet when I stepped out, reminding me more of my parent's ranch than Denver. The sky was a gorgeous blue with streaks of white clouds here and there, the powder around me fresh and enticing. I'd never been much of a skier, but as I watched the guests traveling up and down the length of the lifts, zipping across the white blankets that covered the slopes, I found myself getting the itch.

I pushed all that aside as I made my way toward the huge chalet. People dressed in their winter gear strode in and out, the soft, orange lighting from the windows inviting. One look at the place and its guests made it clear that The Crested Butte Lodge was meant for a certain class of people.

An employee dressed in a classy black uniform smiled at me as I approached, opening the tall, wooden front doors for me. I stepped inside and was greeted with the sight of the gorgeous, bustling lobby, the ceilings tall and complemented with dark wood, massive chandeliers above. The space was big enough to be broken up into several sections, with a large front desk staffed by several people on the right, a lounge to the left, and a bar at the far end. From where I stood, I could see the entrance to an adjoining restaurant, and another door to the equipment rental area. A huge flight of wooden stairs led to the upper floors, flanked by elevators at ground level for those who'd rather travel that way.

It was stunning, pure Colorado luxury and design.

Despite the obvious money on display, there was nothing unapproachable about the lodge. It was the sort of place where you felt warm and cozy just stepping inside, and the groups of people gathered around the many fireplaces sipping coffee and hot cocoa made it clear that was the intention.

But I wasn't there to admire, I was there to work. I opened my bag and slipped out my sketchbook, drawing the place as quickly as I could. I wasn't the best artist in the world, but I was skilled enough to pull off quick mockups for reference purposes. Guests moved around me as I became lost in my own little world of planning, my mind racing with ideas on how to make the already gorgeous space look even more attractive for the event ahead.

"Can I help you?" The words delivered in a professional tone snapped me out of my work trance.

I blinked hard, looking around and trying to find the source of the voice. It didn't take long. To my right was a tall, well-dressed woman in her mid-forties, the expression on her face conveying both warmth and curiosity at who I was and why I was standing in the middle of the entrance area drawing like a madwoman. A gold name tag on her chest read "Tiffany." While she'd greeted me in a friendly manner, I could definitely sense that she was wondering whether or not she was going to have to politely ask me to leave.

"Oh, hi!" I shot out my hand in introduction. "My name's Beth Wheeler. I'm the wedding planner in charge of the Goodjohn-Oliver wedding."

Her eyes lit up with relief at my revelation that I was indeed supposed to be there.

"Oh, right!" she replied. "Miss Wheeler!" She took my

hand and shook it. "So glad you're here. Come along, let me give you a bit of a tour before I take you to the ballroom."

Tiffany proved to be a helpful and knowledgeable guide, informing me about all of the finer points of design in the building.

She talked, I sketched. The place was a wedding planner's dream, with tons of potential for decoration.

"So," she said, taking on a slightly less formal tone as we made our way down the carpeted hallway that led to the ballroom. "This wedding's a pretty big deal, right? I mean, everyone knows the name Goodjohn. Even before they moved their business to New York they were legendary around here."

"Oh, it's going to be a big deal. That's why I'm super excited to plan it. Even though the timing's a little tight."

With that, Tiffany opened the doors into the gorgeous ballroom.

"God, this is something else."

"Isn't it?" Tiffany asked. "It doesn't matter how many times I come into this room, it never fails to blow me away. The ballroom here at Crested Butte is eleven-thousand-five-hundred square feet, with twenty-five-foot-tall ceilings and ten fireplaces."

I went wild sketching as she spoke, my eyes on the windows on either side of the room. The ones to the right looked out over the property, the ones on the left to the mountains. And the three, huge, triangular windows at the back gave a stunning, sweeping view of the valley. It was heaven imagining what kind of altar I'd put there, and how I'd design it.

Tiffany went on, and I couldn't stop smiling as I sketched, totally lost in the fun of designing. It was moments like those that reminded me why I'd gotten into the wedding planning business—to create beautiful spaces where the most wonderful moments of people's lives took place. What could be more satisfying than that?

"Have you seen the view?" Tiffany asked, her eyebrows arched once again.

I tucked my sketchbook under my arm, turning my attention to the big windows at the far end of the room. "How could I miss it? It's amazing!"

Tiffany shook her head. "No, I mean, have you *seen the view*? I'm talking up close and personal."

I was confused. "How do you mean?"

She flashed me a sly smile. "Come here, I'll show you."

Tiffany nodded toward a small door that I hadn't noticed, a bit to the left of the main back area where the altar would be. She opened it, revealing that it led outside. I went over and stepped out, seeing that there was a huge, gorgeous terrace out there big enough for a large crowd of people.

"Nice, huh?" she asked. "Early May can still be a little chilly, but the large space heaters will keep it nice and warm."

"This is so cool," I said. "Totally missed this part when I was here before."

"And like I said, the view is amazing. But you need to go all the way to the edge to really get a sense of it."

She was right about the view. Being outdoors and not looking through a window afforded a sweeping panoramic of the valley. It was so quiet and peaceful out there; no signs of civilization other than the few luxury cabins dotted here and there. It really was hard to believe that we were still pretty close to Denver.

I did as Tiffany suggested, stepping over to the railing and looking down.

"Wow."

Standing that close to the edge, I could see that we weren't just near the valley, we were *over* it. The drop down was hundreds, if not thousands of feet. I was spinning just looking.

"This part of the lodge was built into the side of the mountain. Pretty impressive from an architectural standpoint."

"No kidding. I'll have to warn people not to look down after they've had a few, they might toss their cookies into the valley."

She chuckled. "Anyway, I'm sure you've got a lot you want to see on your own. Let me give you my card—if you have any questions, just send me a text and I'll get back to you ASAP."

Tiffany handed me her card, and I thanked her as she left, turning my attention back to the view. I'd never been crazy about heights, and even though the railing was as secure as it could be, I wanted to get away as quickly as I could.

When I finally stepped away from the ledge, I had to place my hands on the side of one of the many outdoor tables just to give myself a chance to catch my breath.

A tall figure moving around inside the ballroom caught my attention out of the corner of my eye. I looked up to see who it was, but the figure had passed the window as soon as I did.

Probably Beau. Well, better get the reunion over with now, rip that Band-Aid right off.

After one more breath, I strode toward the door and pulled it open.

"Beau, you know you're running a little ear—"

I lifted my eyes, stopping mid step as I realized just who the hell was there.

It wasn't Beau, it was *Jack*.

His eyes flashed at the sight of me, but other than that, he was calm and composed as always. A small smile formed on his impossibly, stupidly handsome face.

"Hey there, gorgeous," he said, his low, bassy voice filling the ballroom. "Long time, no see."

CHAPTER 10

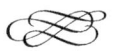

JACK

God*damn* did she look fine.

Didn't matter that she was dressed in a pair of tight jeans and a loose-fitting sweater, her hair done up in a messy bun, it took all the self-control I had not to storm across the ballroom, rip her clothes off, and make her come over and over again right on top of one of the tables.

The attraction was so instant and so intense, in fact, that it overshadowed the fact that the woman I'd slept with a couple months ago was somehow back in my life, standing right in front of me.

"Jack?"

I chuckled. How could I not laugh at the absurdity of the situation? It was really, truly her. And damn, was it surreal. The woman I hadn't been able to get out of my mind was right there in front of me, looking gorgeous as ever.

I stepped over to her slowly, wanting to give her time to process it. The wide-eyed look on her stunning face made it more than obvious she was shocked to see me.

"What are you doing here?"

I cocked my head to the side, leaning against one of the tall, wooden support columns.

"What am I doing here? I'm taking a look at the venue, of course."

"Why?"

I was starting to get pretty damn confused. "Because this is where my son's getting married."

She regarded me with an expression of skeptical confusion, as if not only had what I just said not made a damn bit of sense, but that in the process of saying it, I was trying to pull something over on her.

As we stood silently in that big, grand room, the two of us staring into each other's eyes and trying to figure out what the hell was going on, a thought occurred to me.

"What on earth are *you* doing here?"

Her features softened a bit. "I'm planning the wedding."

I didn't get a chance to ask any more questions before the doors opened, Megan's voice filling the air.

"So, we're going to need this room setup for at least a hundred people. Wedding happens outside, and then we come in here for the party."

Megan strolled in like she owned the place, an expensive purse hanging from the crook of her arm, a pair of designer sunglasses in her hand that she waved around as she spoke.

She stopped once she entered, looking around the big, grand ballroom.

"God, way too much space here. Looks like we're trying too hard to impress." She latched her eyes onto Beth. "Can you do something about this?"

Beth raised her eyebrows, the insanity of the question

seeming to be enough to take her mind off the fact that I was there.

"Uh, do something about what exactly?" she asked.

Megan snorted, as if annoyed. "This room. It's too big."

"Well the room's the same size it was when we met here before."

Megan scoffed. "Yeah, I know. But now that I'm here again, it's just... it's too big."

Right as she finished speaking, Megan's parents entered. I'd been a little ahead of them, having taken a quick phone call with a client that I'd finished just before coming in.

"Don't you think so, Mom?"

"Don't I think so *what*?" her mother replied.

"That the room is too big."

Celina Goodjohn pulled her own pair of designer glasses off her head and looked around, scrunching up her nose as she did.

"It's big. Like we're trying to prove something."

"That's what *I* said," Megan replied.

"I think it's fine," Martin added. "Looks grand."

Megan narrowed her eyes. "Well, you're not the one getting married here. Beth, what can we do about this?"

I chuckled, glancing over at Beau. He shrugged his shoulders, giving me a, "well, what can you do?" sort of look. My eyes went back to Beth, her lips pursed in such a way that gave me the impression she was wondering if she'd gotten herself in over her head.

Damn, she looked sexy and professional all wrapped up into one. It was a hell of a shock seeing her there, but that didn't shake the idea that part of me wished that we were alone so I could have her all to myself one more time. Hell, maybe a few more times.

"You don't *need* to do anything," Celina said, a sharpness to her tone. "Let the guests be impressed when they walk in here. With the money we're spending on this place, I'm fine with showing it off a bit."

"That's *so* low-class, Mom," Megan fired back. "I want to impress people, but I don't want it to *look* like we're trying to impress people."

Beth, through it all, kept a warm, professional smile on her face. What was going on in her mind about me, the wedding and everything else, I could only guess. Celina and Megan settled into their usual bickering, the kind of pecking at one another that I'd heard over and over again that morning.

"I've got an idea," Beth said, cutting them off. The two women stopped their back-and-forth, turning toward Beth.

"Go on," Celina said.

"So, here's what I'm thinking." She hurried over to the entrance, making her way past us. It was impossible not to notice her lovely scent as she passed by, a slight floral aroma lingering in the air. I savored it for the few moments it was there before it dissipated.

She stopped at the entrance and turned around.

"Instead of having the guests walk into the room and get slammed with how huge it is, why don't we set up a little canopy? We make it nice and intimate, maybe add some local flowers—I'm thinking Blanket Flower, Periwinkle, and Pink Mountain Heather for color. Then we slowly open up the canopy, letting it be something like a tunnel, you know? It opens up more and more until, *bam*, they step out and see the windows and the view beyond."

She went on, her mouth spread into a big grin. "So that way, when they finally come out into the room and take it in, they're not thinking about how fancy everything is, at least, not right away. They're too wrapped up in the flowers and the view and all that. Then, when they've had a chance to walk around, have a drink, enjoy the reception, they can let how gorgeous the room itself is sink in."

I had to admit, she was damn good at what she did. More impressive, I had the distinct impression that she was going right off the dome with her ideas, just spinning them up on the spot.

"That could work," Megan said. "But I'd have to see the canopy."

"I could easily sketch something up for you," she said. "Maybe have it ready after lunch? You could all grab a quick bite here, the attached restaurant is amazing."

"As long as they've got a bar," Martin said, "I'm happy."

Celina waved her hand through the air in a dismissive manner.

"Fine," Megan said. "For now, I want to hear more of what you have in mind."

With that, the women settled into conversation, Beth leading them around the room like a pro, directing their attention to the finer points of the space and sharing her ideas for decorating. As the ladies did their thing, Beau, Martin and I found a table to sit where we could kill the time with our own conversation. Most of it was taken up by Martin going on about business in New York, which was fine with me, I wasn't much in the mood for chitchat.

After all, how could I focus on anything when the most beautiful goddamn woman I'd ever seen in my life was just on the other side of the room? I found myself glancing in her direction over and over again, and while I could sense she was trying to stay professional, she couldn't resist flicking her eyes my way every now and then.

An hour flew by. When the ladies were done, the three of them came over to where we were seated.

"You boys ready for lunch?" Megan asked.

"Sure am," Beau said, getting up. "Feel like I could eat a damn elk."

"Hey, give me a little time to drive over to my place," I said, "and I can bring back some of that fresh."

Beau chuckled, shaking his head.

Beth was just to the side of the group, her mouth in a hard, flat line, her cheeks a charming tinge of pin. No doubt she was realizing the time to hide behind work was about to end, and that we were going to have to talk.

She might've been nervous, and I could certainly understand that. I, on the other hand, knew exactly what I wanted. I wanted *her*, and I wanted her all to myself. Not just in a sexual way, though I certainly wanted that.

"Anyway, shall we?" Celina asked. "Beth, you can come with us, if you'd like." Her tone suggested that she was asking out of obligation more than anything else.

"I'm good, thanks," Beth replied. "Our talk gave me some amazing ideas for the room, and I want to sketch them out while they're fresh."

"We'll join you all in a bit," Megan said, wrapping her arm around Beau's. "We wanted to check out the honeymoon suite, see what we have to look forward to." She flicked her eyes over to Beth as soon as she said the words, a sly smirk on her lips. It was strange.

"What about you, Jack?" Martin asked. "Care to knock back a few at the bar? Bet you anything the whiskey selection's as good as it gets."

"Sounds like a fine idea," I said. "But duty calls. Client I spoke with wants to have a lunch meeting. Normally, I can use the bad reception at the cabin to get out of these kinds of things, but I let it slip I was near civilization. So, no such luck."

"Well, when business calls, you have to answer," Martin said. "Next time."

With that, the group made their way out of the room. I hung back, turning just in time to watch as Beth hurried out onto the balcony, sketchbook in hand. I was so eager to see her that I had to hold back from sprinting to the other side of the room.

I opened the door and stepped out into the cool air, Beth sketching wildly at one of the tables, a tall patio heater warming up the area.

"Gimme a sec," she said, her attention totally focused. "If you've got some more questions, we can talk in one minute."

I chuckled, realizing that she'd assumed it was Megan or Celina that had stepped out onto the terrace.

"Just wanted to come and say hey."

She froze mid-sketch when she realized it was me. Beth pursed her lips, her body tense.

"You alright?" I asked.

She came back into the moment, setting down her pencil and pushing away her book.

"Fine," she said, turning to me. "Just fine."

I swept my hand toward the table. "Mind if I join you?"

"Uh, of course."

As I walked over, I realized that I was going to have to be mellow for the both of us.

"That was impressive in there," I said. "You really know your stuff."

"You surprised?" she asked, letting the tension fade a bit from her face and replacing it with a slight smile.

"Not surprised at all, in fact. Anyone would know by

talking to you for two seconds that you're an intelligent woman. Just a pleasure to see it in action." I craned my neck a bit, glancing over at her sketchbook. The drawings had obviously been done quickly but were no doubt dripping with talent. "Good stuff."

The pink tinged her cheeks again, and she closed the book. "Thanks. Just that... I don't like anyone to see them before they're done."

The look on her face was odd, to say the least. Sure, I'd expected her to be a little taken aback by seeing me, just as I was with her. But it was almost as if there were more to it than that.

"Anyway," she said. "I thought you were meeting with a client?"

"Nice thing about working for myself," I said. "I've always got an excuse to get out of doing things I don't want to do. Not to mention, there's no way I'd let you get away without saying hi."

Beth nodded. "This was really unexpected, but... it's good to see you."

"Likewise. In fact, that's part of the reason I came out here to talk to you."

"Oh?"

"Yep. Things are about to get hectic with all the wedding planning, I'm sure. But all the same, I wanted to see if you'd be interested in grabbing some lunch together."

"You... like... on a date?"

"Something like that."

She pursed her lips again. "Here's the thing. I've got, well, I've got a history with Beau."

That was a surprise. "You do? What kind of history?"

"Well, we dated."

"You *what?*" I couldn't keep the surprise out of my

voice. "When?" I asked. I had never heard him mention Beth.

"It was a long time ago, years ago, in fact. Like, back in college."

God, what an admission. I gave myself a minute with it, trying to process.

"How come we never met?" I asked, then realized that might've been a rude question.

She shrugged. "We weren't together all that long. Just a few months really."

I regarded her for a moment before speaking. "Well, isn't that a damn trip?"

"Changes things, doesn't it?" she asked.

"Well, yes and no. Nothing in the world would change the fact that I want to see you again."

"Is that right?" she asked, a small smile spreading.

"That's right. You can't tell me you don't feel the same way."

Beth pursed her lips. "You're right, I can't."

I couldn't resist her for another second. I leaned in, placing my lips on her cheek. Beth didn't fight the kiss, instead she fell into it, her body relaxing, her mouth opening a bit as if she wanted far more than just a kiss on the cheek.

God, her nearness felt good. My cock twitched to life as I pulled my lips away, Beth staying still with a big, broad smile on her face.

"That was nice," she said.

"And it's not going to be the last, gorgeous."

I rose, leaning in and kissing her beautiful face one more time.

"Bye, Jack," she said, smiling at me again before returning to her sketchbook.

I glanced at her as I went back into the ballroom, burning the image of Beth in my mind's eye.

I wasn't sure how to feel about the fact that she'd dated my son. Was I jealous? That didn't seem like the right reaction for a father to have toward his son. All the same, I needed to get my head right about the whole situation because one thing was for certain—I wasn't going to let anyone come between me and getting my hands on Beth again.

CHAPTER 11

BETH

I was breathless as I watched him walk away.

The truth of the matter was that it'd taken all the restraint I'd had not to lean into the kiss and turn my head, letting it land on my lips. Part of me was bothered, sensing that he'd known just what he was doing by kissing me like that, flashing that annoying handsome smile and walking away like everything had gone according to plan.

As I sat there, however, my eyes on the vista before me, I realized that things *hadn't* gone according to plan for him. After all, there was no faking the surprise on his face when I told him that I'd dated his son.

I placed my hand on my belly. *And if he liked that surprise, he's going to* love *the other one I've got in store for him.*

I sighed, sitting back. Regardless of any of it, I needed to get to work. But the fact of the matter was that the brief reunion had left my panties practically soaked through. I got up and walked over to the heater, turning it down a notch; Jack had left me hot enough already.

I went back to the table and opened the sketchbook,

drawing for a bit and trying to focus on work instead of the craziness that had just happened. After getting a few of my best ideas down, I dropped the pencil and sat back, one thought on my mind—what a freaking *mess*. I was planning the wedding of my ex, whose dad happened to give me the best goddamn sex of my life, *and* got me pregnant, all in the same day. It was as if my life had been turned into a cheesy rom-com without my permission.

Work. Get to work. You have all the time in the world to think about this mess you're in. Right now, you need to do the job you're getting paid for, no matter who the client is.

It didn't take long before I was in the zone, drawing like a madwoman again, putting all my ideas down on paper. When I'd poured my brain out onto the page, I sat back, tossed the pencil forward, and sipped my water as I thought it all over.

The canopy was a damn good idea, and the looks on Celina and Megan's faces made it clear they were on board. It'd take some doing, but I was confident that I'd be able to put together the best wedding this place had ever seen.

"How's the grind?"

I turned to see Beau and Megan at the door. Megan's face was flushed, her hair a bit wild. Beau's shirt collar was a bit ruffled, and I was almost positive I could see lipstick underneath.

Gross. Thankfully, the uneasy look on Beau's face suggested he wasn't entirely crazy about a stunt that he'd almost certainly been roped into by his oh-so-lovely fiancée.

"How's our favorite little wedding planner?" Megan asked, Beau's arm draped over her shoulders, his single hand gripped with both of hers.

"Fine, fine," I said, taking my eyes off the couple as

quickly as I could and placing my gaze back onto the sketches. "Just getting some ideas down."

Megan must not have liked me looking away from her, since it didn't take any time at all before she re-entered my field of vision, pulling Beau by the arm.

"*We* had a wonderful time in the honeymoon suite, in case you were wondering. Didn't we, dear?" Beaming, she wrapped Beau's arm around her once more.

"Uh, it was nice. Babe, why don't we freshen up before meeting your parents instead of bothering Beth. She's in the middle of stuff."

"Of course, we had to give the suite a test drive, if you get my meaning." Megan blew past Beau's request, clearly more focused on getting under my skin than anything else.

I wasn't about to let that happen. Maybe high school Beth would have gotten bent out of shape by Megan pulling one of her stupid bits. Grown-ass-woman Beth, on the other hand, was unbothered.

"Oh, aren't you naughty!" I said, flicking my wrist at her. "Boy, I hope you two didn't get caught in 4K by the security cameras in there."

"There were security cameras?" Megan's expression tensed.

"She's just messing with you," Beau said. "Now, why don't we drop the subject of our private life and leave our wedding planner alone to do the job that your parents are paying her a ton of money to do in a very short amount of time?"

"Oh fine," Megan pouted. "I swear, you can be such a buzzkill sometimes, Beau."

Before they had a chance to leave, however, I perked up. A question formed in my mind. Maybe it was a little silly, but I had to ask it, nonetheless.

"Hey, Beau!"

The pair turned. "What's up?" he asked.

"I'm trying to get a sense of what the ceremony itself will look like. What're we thinking about the number of bridesmaids and groomsmen?"

Beau opened his mouth to speak, but Megan beat him to it.

"Four each," she said.

"And are you still thinking about who you want for groomsmen?" I asked Beau.

"*He's* not thinking about anything," Megan said. "Not a single person is going to participate in this wedding unless I approve."

Beau shrugged, giving a sheepish little smile that suggested that she'd laid down the law.

"OK, that works," I replied, pushing my thoughts on the budding Bridezilla aside. "Now, how about walking down the aisle? Your dad's going to walk you, Megan?"

"Right."

"And we'll have to figure out who's going to walk your mom down the aisle. Remember, the bride's mother is the last to be seated before the ceremony begins, so that's something to think about."

"Got it."

I paused for a moment as I approached the topic that was really on my mind.

"And how about your dad, Beau?" I asked. "Is there a... certain someone in his life? Didn't see a ring, but maybe a girlfriend?"

Beau let out a sharp laugh at my words.

"What?" I asked. "Am I missing something?"

He shook his head. "No, sorry, it's a totally reasonable question. Just that... Dad doesn't date."

"Huh?" I wasn't sure what to make of this considering he'd asked me to lunch not thirty minutes earlier. "He doesn't date?"

"Dad, well, he lives something of an unusual lifestyle."

I knew just what he meant, of course, but I had to play dumb.

"What do you mean?"

Megan leaned forward, her eyes flashing, a grin on her face. "He lives in the freaking *woods*. Can you believe it? He's out there all by himself with his dog."

"Like, in a cabin?"

"Yep," she said, evidently continuing to answer questions for her fiancé. "I mean, don't get me wrong—it's a *nice* cabin, total luxury situation. In fact, I wouldn't mind having something like that in the mountains for weekend getaways, hint-hint." She playfully nudged Beau, though no doubt she was laying the groundwork for expecting a mountain getaway as a gift in the coming years.

"He moved to the cabin when I started college," Beau said. He likes his solitude and he never really dated after my mom died."

Megan's eyes lit up again. "It's so sad that someone as handsome as your dad never got back out there. A guy like him? Sexy and rich and just the right amount of silver fox? God, even *I* wonder if I have a little crush on him sometimes."

"Megs," Beau said. "That's my *dad* you're talking about."

"What?" she asked, shrugging her shoulders. "I'm just saying that if he'd put himself out on the market, he'd find someone like *that*." she snapped her fingers as she said the word.

"So, let me get this straight," I said. "Not only is he not

dating anyone, but he's also never dated anyone? I mean since your mom?"

"What does this have to do with the wedding again?" Megan asked, clearly getting a little annoyed that she and her special day weren't the topic of conversation.

"Nope," Beau said, answering my question and not hers. "Just him and Buddy."

I was getting tenser by the minute, the topic of Jack tying me in knots. How the hell would these two react if they were to learn that I was pregnant with his freaking kid? And I wasn't even going to *think* about the possibility that I very well could've been the first woman he'd been with since Beau's mom died.

I needed to be alone, to sit and process everything I'd just learned.

"Uh, anyway!" I said. "That should be it for now. Thanks!"

"Um, sure," Megan said. Her tone made it clear that she'd noticed the abrupt way I'd ended the conversation. "Let's go, Mom and Dad are waiting down in the restaurant."

"Yeah, sounds good. See you, Beth. Let us know if you need anything else."

"Will do."

With that, the two of them left the terrace and headed inside. I sat there for a moment, trying to work through the massive, complicated problem I had on my lap. I *needed* this wedding—not just for the huge payday that awaited me, but for the future success it'd all but ensure if I managed to pull it off.

At the same time, the situation with Beau and Jack, me and the baby, was no small thing. I needed to come clean, but doing so would throw everything into turmoil—not only could it ruin the wedding, but it would also almost certainly ruin my career. After all, what couple would want to hire the wedding planner that screwed the groom's dad?

The longer I sat with it, the more I realized there was only one thing to do—I had to tell Jack about the baby. After a few more minutes of thinking it over, I grabbed my book and bag and headed inside, making my way through the event room and into the hall, then to the lobby.

Once there, I spotted Beau and Megan in front of the restaurant, their backs toward me as they seemed to be having an argument. I passed them quietly, not wanting to get their attention. However, the closer I got, the more I could hear what they were saying.

"She's still so weird, isn't she?" Megan asked. "I mean, I don't want to sound like a bitch, but it's almost like she's still the same awkward little weirdo she was in high school."

"Come on babe," Beau replied. "She's fine. And I did date that 'awkward little weirdo,' so ease up."

"God don't remind me. I'm still frustrated we had to go with her for the wedding. She's lucky that everyone else is booked up."

"You're saying that like she's not talented," Beau replied. "You saw those samples from those other two weddings she did. Beth's a hidden gem. I bet you anything two years from now she's going to be *the* wedding planner in Denver. She's always been talented like that."

Megan scoffed. "You ask me, it's weird the way you still defend her. The normal thing to do is trash-talk all your exes. You know, like I do." She followed these words up with a laugh at her own joke.

"Oh, you want to talk about weird? How about the way you always mention how hot you think my dad is, especially in front of mixed company."

Another laugh. "What, you jealous?"

"I'm not jealous of my own damn father. But it's more than a little inappropriate."

"Oh, whatever, stop being so sensitive. Anyway, I'm serious about Megan. If she does a good job with the wedding, great. But if I even get a *hint* that she's screwing this up for me, she's out. And I'll make damn sure that she never plans a wedding again—*ever*."

With that, they settled into standard couple bickering. I snuck past, making sure they didn't realize I was right behind them. Once I was outside, I hurried to my car and started the engine. Mom and Dad's ranch was an hour away, and from there it'd be a little longer to Jack's cabin. I didn't have the exact address, but I was sure with a little effort I could find it.

I had to—we needed to talk, and soon.

CHAPTER 12

JACK

The weather was warm enough that I needed to pull off my flannel as I worked hacking away at the old red oak I'd picked. We were getting to the end of winter, but March always seemed to have a way of surprising you with a final slam of snow at the tail end of the season. Forecast was looking intense for the next few days, and I aimed to be ready.

As I worked, I couldn't stop thinking about Beth.

Usually, swinging the axe helped to take my mind off of things, but that time it wasn't working. The more I worked, the more I kept thinking about her. She'd flash into my mind in all different kinds of scenarios, from her naked and moaning underneath me, to her back at the lodge dressed in a sweater and jeans. Didn't matter what she was wearing or what the circumstances were, she was still the most beautiful damn thing I'd ever seen in my life.

My attraction to Beth was complicated enough. That was only part of the problem, there was also guilt. Though I'd had one-nighters to scratch the physical itch over the years, Beth had been the first woman I'd felt anything for since Charlotte passed. Allowing myself to feel so drawn to someone else seemed like a betrayal, even though it had been several years.

All those thoughts were swimming in my mind as I thwacked the axe into a large log. The big piece split in two, the sound echoing through the woods. When I was done, I plunged my axe into the stump and took a deep breath, wiping my brow with the back of my hand as I looked out onto the woods. The sky was clear and crisp, the air tinged with that sort of alpine freshness you only seemed to find in the Rockies. Buddy was sleeping at the base of a nearby tree, whimpering and kicking his leg as he dreamed of chasing birds.

A beer sure as hell sounded good. I headed inside, opened up the fridge and pulled out a Coors, holding it to my head as I went out back. The view was killer on the other side of the property, a nice, sweeping vista of the forest and mountains. I cracked my beer and took a long sip, finding my mind drifting to memories long passed...

I remembered the day Charlotte passed like it was last week. I'd been in San Francisco for work. I was sitting in a tower office downtown across from my client at the time—this rich guy who'd inherited a shit-ton of money from his parents and wanted to know how to spend it. More specifically, he'd wanted to know how to turn it into even more money. I'd been happy to oblige; wouldn't have been the first fortune I'd doubled or even tripled.

Charlotte was back home in Denver with Beau, who was three-and-a-half-months-old. I was still adjusting to parenthood, still trying to wrap my head around this whole "being responsible for another life" thing. I'd hated to have to leave town, but Charlotte had her parents, and money was money.

It'd all started with my client receiving a phone call. He had been in the middle of talking about an idea to invest, and I'd been trying to talk him out of it.

"Amanda, you *know* not to call me in the middle of a meeting. I'm serious…"

He went on, chewing out his secretary. As he did, I found myself looking out the window at the city and the bay in the distance, a small smile forming on my lips at the idea of seeing Charlotte and Beau again. I hated to be apart from them, even for a little while, but I knew the longing I felt would only make seeing them again all the sweeter.

"Why didn't you say it was an emergency? For Jack? Yeah, he's right here." My client handed me the phone. Instantly I became filled with dread. I *knew* something was wrong.

I took the phone and slowly brought it to my ear. The assistant told me that a hospital in Denver was on the line, and she'd patch me though.

A nurse was on the line within seconds. There'd been an accident, the car sliding on black ice, Charlotte and Beau inside. My world spun around me as I stood up and held onto the back of the chair for support. Beau was fine, thank God, but Charlotte…

Within an hour, I was on a flight back to Denver. I drove to the hospital like a madman, the world still swirling and blurry around me as if I were underwater. When I arrived at the hospital I rushed inside, my heart pounding.

I knew the instant I saw her parents, saw the looks on their faces, that she was gone, that I'd been too late.

The moment I realized that Charlotte was dead and that I didn't even get to say goodbye felt like my heart had been pulled right from my chest, a wound forming I knew would leave scar tissue that would never go away.

Thank God above, Beau was fine. I dropped to my knees in relief and gratitude when I saw him in that hospital crib, my son crying, no clue that he'd never get to know his mother.

The weeks following were a blur. Family arrived to take some of the load off my shoulders, to help me plan and watch over my boy. The clearest memory I had from those strange, surreal days after I'd lost the love of my life was during the funeral, holding Beau as he slept, realizing that it was all on me. Despite the sadness I carried, despite my uncertainty in my abilities as a father, it was all on me.

Buddy barked, bringing me back into the moment. I'd been so lost in my thoughts that my beer had gone warm in my hand. I sipped it, thinking about how I'd made the decision not to date at all after Charlotte passed, after I'd had some time to grow accustomed to my new life. It didn't seem right to see anyone else. Not to mention how confusing that'd be for poor Beau, and how I couldn't even imagine opening my heart for someone who wasn't my wife.

Until Beth, that is. I'd laid eyes on her that first time and known there was something different about her, something special. I'd have to tell Beau that she and I had something, no matter how strange it might be for him to know I'd gone and fallen for his ex-girlfriend.

Buddy let out another bark, alerting me to something. I took another swig of my beer, making my way around the house.

"Buddy!" I called out. "This better not be you yapping at shadows, big guy!"

The second I turned the corner around the cabin, I realized that wasn't the case.

A man in a sharp suit stood in front of an expensive car, a sinister smile on his face.

He was no stranger. No, this was a man from my past, a man I'd hoped to never see again.

"Afternoon, Jacky. Got a second to chat with an old pal?"

CHAPTER 13

JACK

Michael fucking Schafer. If there was a man I never wanted to see again, it was him.

Michael was dressed in his usual three-piece suit, with gaudy gold chains and two matching pinky rings coated with diamonds. The man was loaded, and liked to make sure everyone who was unlucky enough to meet him knew it. He was big, tall as he was wide, with slicked-back blonde hair thinning and going white. His face was fleshy, his eyes sunken and dark, his skin pale and wrinkled.

Then there was that smile, that horrible, jagged smile that always reminded me of the grin of a Jack O' Lantern. I knew enough of his history to understand just how evil he was. I'd worked with the guy for years, after all.

"Jacky," he said, shaking his head. "God, it's good to see you." Michael stood in front of his car, a late-model luxury ride as dark as midnight. A little dust had gathered around the tires, and there was no doubt that he'd have that cleaned off the moment he was back in town. A man in dark sunglasses sat in the driver's seat, no doubt armed.

"Gotta be honest, Michael, not happy to see you in the slightest."

Michael made a put-on sad face, one that stretched his already unattractive features into something even worse.

"Oh, you're breaking my heart. I drive all the way up to the city to find you, not to mention go to the *immense* trouble of finding where you're hanging your hat these days—and this is how you greet me?"

"It sure as hell is. And if your feelings are hurt because I'm not rolling out the welcome wagon for you, you're more than welcome to hop back in that overpriced ride of yours and have your little helper take you back to Denver."

Michael ignored my words, putting his hands on his hips and looking over my place.

"Very nice, Jacky. Can't help but notice that, while you're so very rude to me, you've been more than happy to build yourself a charming little place with the money you no doubt earned working for me."

"Didn't earn it all working for you." The words felt hollow as I said them; he had me dead to rights.

He laughed. "Don't even try that horseshit with me, my friend. I remember where you were when I found you, barely making a living off paltry investment fees from bored rich kids with money to throw around. You were struggling to get by, struggling to make a future for you and that boy of yours."

I raised my finger, pointing to the wood-chopping axe nestled in the stump.

"See that tool over there?" I asked. "Now, unless you want to find out if you can get in that car faster than it takes for me to grab it and split you like firewood, you'll not even *think* about mentioning my boy, understand?"

Michael laughed again. "You were always hot under the

collar, Jacky—one of the reasons I was so keen on you from the get-go."

I shifted my weight from one foot to another, knowing that Michael wasn't going to leave until he'd said whatever he'd come to tell me.

"What do you want, Michael?" I asked.

"Now, was that so hard, being polite? How about this—you and I head inside this nice place of yours, you give me one of those beers, and we talk about what I came here to discuss. Sound fair?"

"Fine. Whatever gets you off my land the fastest."

I turned, throwing open the door and heading inside. Once there, I grabbed a white T-shirt off the back of a chair in the living room, Michael following me inside.

"This is some place," he said, stepping over the threshold and looking around. "You're in the woods, got your peace and quiet, but still know how to live."

"Sit," I said, pointing to one of the chairs in the living room. "I'll get your beer."

"Much obliged, Jacky."

I went into the kitchen, grabbed a beer out of the fridge and returned to the living room, tossing it to Michael. He neatly caught it, showing a surprising bit of agility for a man of his age and state of fitness. It was a reminder that he was no one to screw around with; the man was deadly.

He cracked the beer and took a swig, letting out a long, slow *ahh* after swallowing then holding the can in front of his face and shaking his head.

"I've drank some of the finest, most expensive booze on God's green earth, Jacky, some of it with you, if you remember. But sometimes nothing tastes better than a humble domestic in an aluminum can."

I leaned against the wall, my arms crossed over my chest.

"Tell me what you want."

"Why don't you have a seat, first? Making me antsy with you standing over there."

He was playing games, trying to say without saying that the meeting began and ended on his terms. All the same, I dropped into the armchair across from him, making sure the front door was visible out of the corner of my eye.

"Oh, don't worry about that," he said, waving his hand dismissively. "If I wanted you dead, I'd have done it with a silenced rifle from somewhere in the forest while you were chopping wood. Would never have known what hit you." He grinned and winked, giving me a moment to let that sink in. "You're safe."

"Forgive me if I'm being skeptical," I said, a sardonic tone to my words. "But I've seen what you do to people facing you, let alone with their backs to you."

"Well, you're going to have to trust me when I say that's not why I'm here. Stop being so paranoid. Besides, harming that brilliant brain of yours is the last thing I want—what you've got in your skull is too valuable to put a bullet through."

"Then get to it."

Another smile. "The long and short of it is that I need someone with your numerical skills to work some magic."

"Why? I thought when I was done working with you your crew had hired a whole team of number crunchers to take care of your finances."

"We did. But we soon learned that a dozen crooked CPAs looking to make a little something under the table were nothing compared to one Jack Oliver. They're fine for the day-to-day, but what we've got going on now is out of the ordinary."

"I'm nothing special," I said flatly.

He went on as if I hadn't spoken. "This nosy little FBI bitch named Amy Miller has been poking around our operations. She's wet behind the ears, trying to make a name for herself coming after us. Got a feeling it's only a matter of time before she tries to take us down using the IRS."

"And that's where I come in. Let me guess—you want me to go over the numbers for you, make sure everything looks nice and legit in case an audit comes down the pipe."

Michael took another sip of his beer, flicking his eyebrows up. "You got it."

"You know that I'm done with this bullshit, right? We cut ties, and that was the end of it."

"You did tell me that. I have very specific memories of that particular conversation along with all the choice words you shot in my direction. Don't worry, I don't hold grudges." He swept his hand over his shoulder. "Like water off a duck's feathered back."

He leaned forward. "But you must remember the first rule—you're *never* out, not for good. We need you, and you're going to work for us again."

"And why the hell would I do that?"

He let out a dismissive snort, shaking his head. "Come on now. You do this for me, for my organization, and there's a solid payday in it for you."

"I don't need money."

"*Everyone* needs money." He reached into his jacket pocket and took out a pen and piece of paper, jotting something down before ripping the piece off and handing it over. "And you can't tell me you're going to say no to this kind of offer."

I took the paper and flipped it over. The amount was impressive, enough to give me pause. All the same, I shook my head, tossing the piece of paper onto the coffee table.

"Don't need it. Peace of mind is more valuable than that."

Michael grinned, as if he'd been expecting that kind of answer.

"Fine. Double it. And please offer my sincere congratulations to your Beau, getting married to that gorgeous Megan girl. A bit of a pill from what I've seen, but the wedding you're all planning at the Crested Butte Lodge should be something to remember."

Anger boiled inside of me at his words. They might've been delivered with a friendly tone, but the implicit threat was clear.

"You touch so much as a hair on his head and I'll kill you my damn self."

"You take the money, you do the job, and we won't need to worry about any of that sordid business. Come on, you can't tell me that sitting up here doing independent contractor business now and then is really scratching the itch."

I sat in pure anger for several long moments. I wanted to rip that ugly fucker apart for threatening my family.

As much as I hated it, there was nothing to do other than to agree. Michael had power and money and wasn't afraid to kill to get what he wanted. I couldn't let anything happen to my son.

"I know this is a risk," he went on. "There's a good chance you'll be in the crosshairs of the FBI. But you being you, you'll get the job done staying under the radar and without raising any red flags. Just agree, Jacky. Say yes and the money's yours, and I'll be out of your hair—for the time being, at least."

Right as he finished his sentence, I heard the sound of a car door shutting in front of the house.

"Expecting company?" he asked.

"Nope." I got up and went over to the window. My stomach sank at what I saw.

Beth stepped out of the car looking as gorgeous as she had earlier. Buddy ran up to her, happily jumping up on her legs. She laughed, petting him as she made her way to the front door. Michael rose, going over to one of the other windows.

"Now that's a good-looking woman. Does this mean you've finally gotten over her, Jacky? I swear, all those beautiful women I dangled in front of your face when we worked together, not a single one did anything for you."

My heart beat quicker, my blood running hot.

"Leave *now*," I said, turning to Michael.

Michael laughed. "Of course, of course. I wouldn't dream of standing between you and your lady, Jacky. Here's the deal—you keep an eye out for an email that will have your instructions, should be arriving to your inbox very soon. And don't worry, it'll be encrypted."

A knock sounded at the door, and Michael smiled.

"I'll see myself out."

He stepped over to the door, but I beat him to it.

"Hey!" Beth said. "Sorry to drop in unannounced like this, especially since you have company. You want me to come back later?"

"No, no, no," Michael said. "I was just leaving." He took her hand, placing a kiss on top of it. I wanted to punch his ugly face right then and there. Hell, I wanted to do worse than that. Instinct took over and I put my hand on Beth's arm, pulling her away and wrapping my arm around her shoulders.

Michael glanced at me, no doubt seeing the anger on my face at him touching Beth. I realized right away that I'd made a mistake by letting him see that she meant something to me.

"Keep an eye out for that email," he said. "We'll be in touch soon."

He stepped around Beth, making his way to his car and flashing me one more smile before getting in, a smile that made it clear beyond a shadow of a doubt that he wasn't done with me yet.

CHAPTER 14

BETH

To say I was uncomfortable at the strange man's touch would've been the understatement of the decade. Everything about him screamed untrustworthy and threatening. Jack and I said nothing as we watched and waited for the man to leave.

"Fuckin' prick," Jack snarled. There was pure venom in his voice, an anger that nearly made me uneasy.

"Sorry," I said finally, once the man was gone. "I shouldn't have come here unannounced."

Jack shook his head, his eyes still on the horizon as if he wanted to make damn sure that the man was long gone. When he was satisfied, he turned to me and closed the door.

"You're fine, don't need to apologize for anything."

Little by little, I began to feel better, as if whatever danger had been present was gone. The increased mental space gave me the chance to appreciate Jack in front of me, how goddamn good he looked in that thin, skintight, V-neck white T-shirt. The fabric clung to his body, the V of the collar drawing attention to his solid, square pecs. It didn't take much ogling before I felt myself clench, arousal building by the second.

His physical presence was so overwhelming that I had to shake my head to come back to reality.

"You alright there?" he asked. Jack put his big, strong hands on my shoulders, which didn't help matters.

"Uh, fine. Just fine."

He let out an amused chuckle as he took his hands away.

"I'm drinking a beer," he said, turning and making his way over to one of the two cans in the living room. "You want one?" He plucked both of the cans from where they were, tossing one in a nearby trash can and pulling a long sip of the other.

"Nah, just water."

"Suit yourself."

He disappeared into the kitchen. Once he was gone, I took a moment to look around the cabin again. I loved it, the furniture and accoutrements a perfect blend of modern and handmade—the perfect bachelor pad for a man who enjoyed living on his own and keeping to himself. I even noticed a few pictures of Beau on the walls, and I couldn't help but shake my head at how much less complicated things could've been if I'd noticed those before.

Jack returned a few moments later with a bottle of water. He tossed it to me and I caught it, opening the cap and taking a slow sip. As I drank, I thought about the anger that I'd heard in Jack's voice, the rage flashing in his eyes. I wanted to know what had gone down, but knew it wasn't my place to question.

All the same, I had to ask. "You OK?"

"Huh?" he took a sip of his beer, as if giving himself a few seconds to come up with an answer that wouldn't reveal too much. "Oh. Yeah, I'm fine. Don't worry about me." I allowed myself a smile at this. What else could I have expected from a man like Jack?

"Come over and sit down." He nodded to the couch, the same one where we'd made love that first night.

I sat down on it, the softness of the cushion and the view of the fireplace bringing all sorts of sexy memories back. When Jack sat next to me, his earthy, musky scent filling the air, I found it extremely hard to think about anything other than how much I wanted him to pin me down and make me come over and over again.

"Now," he said, draping his big, thick arm over the back of the couch behind me. "As nice as it is for you to drop in, I gotta admit I'm curious what brings you to my neck of the woods."

"Sorry." I shook my head again, trying to come to my senses. "I promise there is a legitimate reason for just showing up like this."

He chuckled, taking one more sip of his beer before setting it down on the coffee table.

"Well, while you gather your thoughts, can I tell you what's on my mind?" He flashed me a small smile, one that went a long way in putting my mind at ease. There was something about Jack that never failed to make me feel warm and safe and sexual all at the same time.

"Sure."

He leaned toward me. "I was just thinking that if you don't stop staring at me with that look in your eyes, I'm going to give you more of what you got the first time we met."

My eyes flashed with total surprise, my heart skipping a beat. He continued to look at me, hunger in his gaze.

Despite the entanglements between us, I was turned on

like mad. I wanted exactly what he was offering, and I wanted it right then and there. Instead of saying anything at all, I stared at him with my mouth opened slightly. My panties were soaked through, my body yearning for him.

Jack reached over, putting his big hand on the back of my neck and gently guiding us closer together.

"Tell me, Beth, is this what you want?" he spoke low, his eyes locked on mine. Just like our first night together, he was giving me an out. And just like our first night together, he knew exactly what I wanted.

"Yes. Yes, it is."

He leaned in and kissed me, the sensation of his lips on mine so intense that I felt like I was having an out-of-body experience in the best way possible. I opened my mouth, his tongue passing my lips and finding mine. He tasted so, *so* damn good, the tang of beer on his tongue as his beard brushed against the softness of my cheeks.

I decided to go for what had been on my mind since I'd first laid eyes on him. I grabbed on to the hem of his shirt and pulled it up over his head, exposing the powerful upper body underneath. His muscular physique was enough to make me feel like a dam had broken down below.

Jack began working on my clothes, pulling my sweater off over my head and tossing it aside. The bra I had on underneath was nothing special, just a simple black racerback that was my go-to bra whenever I didn't want to think about what to wear. The look in Jack's eyes, however, made me feel like it was the sexiest damn thing he could imagine.

"You're something else, you know that gorgeous?"

I couldn't help but grin. "You're not so bad yourself."

We went full force at one another's clothes. I opened his belt and zipper as he kicked off his work boots. After a little bit of team effort, we had one another down to our underwear. Jack flicked his eyes up and down me one more time, shaking his head as if in disbelief.

Then he pounced.

He pinned me down, kissing me hard before reaching around and pulling off my bra, my nipples going hard as soon as they were exposed to the air of the cabin and the anticipation of Jack's touch. He leaned down and put his mouth on one breast, then the other. I sighed, closing my eyes and savoring the feeling of his tongue on my nipples, the sensation enough to make me begin to feel the first stirrings of an orgasm.

When he'd had his fun with my breasts, Jack backed off and stood up. The way he looked looming over me in nothing but his boxer briefs, his big, thick cock straining against the fabric, his muscles covered with sweat, was enough to make my heart feel as if it might explode out of my chest.

"Stand up." His voice was powerful, commanding. I obeyed as if I were in a trance, totally wrapped up in his looks and his voice and his scent and everything else.

Even on my feet, he was still imposingly tall before me.

"Take off your panties. And keep your eyes on mine while you do it."

I did as he asked, pulling them down my legs and kicking them off, never once breaking eye contact with him. When I stood back up straight, I was totally bare and exposed in front of him. His eyes moved slowly up and down my body, as if he wanted to burn every detail of me into his mind.

Finally, he stepped forward. One of his big hands went to the curve of my hip, the other to my inner thigh. I gasped as he touched me, the sensation so intense that I could hardly think straight.

"Now," he said, inching his hand up closer and closer to my pussy. "We're in my house. That means you follow my rules. With me so far?"

Of course, he chose that moment to touch me, the sensation enough to make me gasp, my knees to buckle a bit.

"I'm with you." I moaned, pressing myself against his touch.

"Good. There are two rules, so listen closely. First is you do what I say." He parted my lips with his fingertips, moving one inside of me. I moaned again, leaning forward and putting my head against his chest. The dusting of chest hair on his pecs made for the perfect pillow.

"Got it." I moaned again, his thumb pressing against my clit.

"The second is that you only come when I give you permission. Understand?"

"Y...yes..." I was so lost in the pleasure of his touch that his words seemed distant and dreamy. Pleasure built with surprising speed and intensity, an orgasm almost within reach.

Jack placed his hand on my chin and tilted my face up. I opened my eyes to see his handsome face gazing down at me.

"Say 'I understand.'"

My legs were starting to shake, the climax growing closer and closer the more he touched me. But there was something about his voice and tone, commanding and intense, that rapidly brought me to the verge of release.

"I understand."

"Good," he replied. "Now, I want you to come for me."

As if he'd cast a magic spell on me, his words pushed me over the brink, an orgasm ripping through my body as he fingered me. I threw my head back and let out a cry,

Jack wrapping his arm around my waist and pulling me close, holding me upright as he continued to stroke my swollen clit. Pleasure ripped through me, the sensation of his hard, powerful body against mine only increasing its intensity.

When the orgasm faded, Jack put his hands on my hips and moved in to kiss me. I opened my mouth, his tongue moving slowly past my lips, his cock pressing against my stomach.

"I need it," I sighed. "Please."

He grinned, as if he'd been waiting to hear those words.

"Get on the couch and turn around."

I did as he directed, climbing onto the couch and placing my arms along the back. I turned to watch him approach, and he spoke as I did so.

"Keep your eyes forward."

I grinned, something about the way he commanded me sending shivers up my spine. I turned my attention ahead, the window before me looking out onto the woods. I felt Jack's hand on my back as he removed his boxer briefs, the head of his cock brushing against my rear.

I shivered again as I felt the tip of his manhood press against my lips. I wanted desperately to turn around, to watch him as he moved into me. More than that, however, I wanted to please him, to do exactly as he'd instructed.

Jack pushed inside of me, his thickness spreading my lips and stretching my walls. Once more, my body shook at his touch, this time the intensity so great that I found myself gripping the back of the couch for support.

"God, that feels *so* good." The words flowed out of me as he pushed the last few inches of his thickness deep inside.

"And you feel like heaven, baby," he said. Jack moved

his hand over my back, then along the curve of my hip. "You're so beautiful, you know that?"

He followed up his words by pulling his hips back and pushing into me. Just like the first time, he moved slowly, allowing me to adjust to his thickness and length. I squirmed against him, pushing my ass toward his body, making sure that every last bit of him vanished inside me. Once he'd given me a chance to adjust, Jack picked up the pace of his thrusting, his cock moving in and out of me like a piston, quickly pushing me to the brink of another orgasm.

He began to buck harder, fast enough to make my breasts swing back and forth underneath me, my nails digging into the cushion. Each deep, full penetration of his cock was another layer of total ecstasy, and it didn't take long before I was once more on the verge of coming.

"I'm gonna... I'm..." I trailed off as I spoke, as if reciting a chant.

"You're not doing anything until I say so."

I closed my eyes, once more sinking into the force and weight of his command. I let the pleasure build even more, backing up like water against a dam ready to burst. It built and built until finally I couldn't take it anymore.

"Please," I moaned. "Please let me come."

"Do it."

I let out a scream as I gave myself over to the climax, the second one so intense that it made the previous one seem like nothing at all. I gripped the back of the couch so hard that I worried I might tear the fabric. Jack kept pounding me all the while, the pace of his thrusts unrelenting in the best way possible.

When my orgasm was over, I let my head hang down. Jack reached around me and scooped me up, carrying my body fireman style as if I weighed nothing at all. He carried me out of the living room and down the hall, into a huge master bedroom with a large wood-framed bed and a killer view of the valley behind the cabin.

Once there, he laid me down on the bed on my back and moved over top of me. I was practically delirious from the pleasure but even so, I took the chance to admire his gorgeous form, his long, thick cock pointing straight down.

He wrapped one arm around me, using his other hand to guide his cock between my legs. The first two orgasms had nearly knocked me into another dimension, but all the same one more sounded like heaven. I opened my legs and wrapped them around his hips, Jack sliding his cock inside and filling me with his solid warmth.

He moved in and out, and it didn't take much time at all before we were both on the brink of coming. The way his face tightened with pleasure, his grunts becoming deeper and harder, let me know he was on the verge of release.

"Come with me," he commanded. "Now."

I did, and he was right there with me. The final orgasm was like hot liquid moving through my body, the pleasure accompanied by Jack's release, his body tensing as his cock erupted deep inside. I savored it all, holding his body against mine, my breasts pressed against his chest.

When we were done, he held me close, my head on his chest as it rose and fell. There was one thing on my mind, however, that I knew I had to tell him about sooner than later—our baby inside of me.

CHAPTER 15

BETH

All I could do after was stare at the ceiling, bathing in the afterglow, amazed by what had just happened.

Jack had stepped out to grab some water, leaving me alone with my thoughts for a few moments. I let my eyes trace over the wood ceiling above, the support clearly hand-carved. I wouldn't have been surprised if he'd built this whole damn place himself.

It wasn't long before he sauntered back into the room, not a stitch of clothing on him. He walked with total confidence, his thick cock between his powerful thighs, a water bottle in his hand.

"Here," he said. "You're probably thirsty as hell too."

Looking at his gorgeous body on full display in front of me, "thirsty" was certainly the right word. He handed me the water and I drank, nearly draining the entire bottle. When I was done, I set it aside just in time for him to move in and greet me with another deep kiss.

Just like that, I was ready to go again. I stopped myself, however, putting my hands on his big shoulders and gently pushing him away. He moved back, a slightly curious look on his face.

"Something up?"

"Kind of. I just have something I want to talk to you about."

He nodded, seeming unbothered by my sudden change in attitude. It was something I really liked about Jack, how unflappable he was, how nothing seemed to get under his skin or make him lose his cool. That is, aside from a strange man in an expensive suit kissing my hand.

He offered me his hand and together, we went back to the living room. I dressed, watching Jack slip into his jeans and that tight, white T-shirt. He plopped onto the couch, reaching for the beer he'd been drinking before our fun.

"Listen, it's obvious you're worried."

"Am I really that readable?"

"You're clearly tense. Are you worried about Beau, about what he'd think if he were to find out about what was going on between us?"

"I mean, I guess a little? We weren't together all that long or super serious, but I just don't want anything to come between you two if he feels weird about it."

Just like always, Jack didn't seem too concerned. "Beau's got a lot going on these days. But he's a grown man, he can handle what life throws at him. And if we end up dating, then he's going to have to be OK with that."

I opened my mouth to speak. As soon as I processed his words, however, I paused, my eyes flashing wide.

"Wait, did you just say you wanted to *date*?"

"I sure as hell did." There wasn't the slightest hesitation to his voice. He knew what he wanted, and he wasn't afraid to put it out there. "Beth, the way I feel about you... I can't explain it. You're brilliant and gorgeous and ambitious, definitely talented from what little I've seen. I've wrestled with this feeling for a good long while, basically the whole damn time since we first met. But seeing you today got me thinking that there might be something deeper going on."

"Something deeper?"

"Yeah. I know this is going to sound corny as all hell, but it feels like we were meant to meet, for something to happen between us."

He reached over and took my hand. As Jack regarded me with those warm, sensual eyes, it became beyond clear to me that I had to tell him right then and there about the baby. I knew it was going to be the hardest thing I'd ever had to say.

"The wedding's going to be a huge production, and Megan isn't the easiest person in the world to deal with. Throwing the fact that we're dating into the mix might cause a fight or two, but—"

"I'm pregnant."

It was far from the most elegant or diplomatic way to break the news. But I knew that if I danced around the issue for too long or tried to say it in the perfect way, it'd never get out.

"You're... what?" He cocked his head to the side.

"I'm pregnant." The second time was easier than the first, coming out with a little more confidence. "I'm pregnant, and it's yours."

The confused look stayed on his face. "You're pregnant?"

"I am."

He formed his lips into a thin line, looking out the window. Jack was totally stupefied—as if part of his brain had suddenly been sucked out of his head.

He stood up and made his way slowly over to the

window. Once there, he put his hands on the windowsill and looked out over the back stretch of his property.

After a time, he spoke. "You're... *pregnant?*"

"Listen, Jack. I know this is a lot to process. Trust me, I totally get that. But the fact of the matter is that I'm pregnant and I need to know what you think about it. I am keeping the baby and if you want to be in his or her life, that's great. If not, I'll deal with that too. But I need to know."

Jack said nothing at first, his back still to me. For a moment, I was worried that he'd gone into shock or something.

Finally, he turned around, the confusion gone, replaced by determination. He stepped over to me and took my hands into his.

"Listen here, you're out of your mind if you don't think I'm going to raise this kid with you."

Now it was my turn to be stunned.

CHAPTER 16

JACK

However stunned I was a few moments ago, Beth was that—times ten.

"You... *what*?" she asked, her eyes wide.

"You heard me. If you're pregnant, if you want to have this baby, then I'm right here with you." Her hands still in mine, I brought her over to the couch and sat her down next to me.

"Look, you just knocked me on my ass. Here I've been going back and forth on the subject of you and I openly dating, and now you're telling me there's a baby in the picture—that's a hell of a thing you just put on my lap."

"I know. And I'm sorry."

"Sorry for what?"

"I don't know. Throwing your life into a tizzy? I mean, I know how it feels. I only found out myself today."

I laughed. "Is that right?"

She smiled a wary, apprehensive smile. "So... you're not mad?"

"How the hell could I be mad? Beth, this is a baby we're

talking about here. Now, I'm speaking from experience that you don't have, but there's nothing more incredible than holding your own child for the first time moments after he's come into the world, looking at that little face and knowing you created it."

I couldn't help but smile, thinking back to the day that Beau came into the world. My happiness must've been contagious, as Beth was smiling right there with me.

"Anyway," I went on. "I was telling you that I was feeling our paths might've been destined to cross. What you've just said only makes me feel more certain about that."

"Are you sure?" she asked. "It's just that I don't want you to feel like you've been pushed into a corner."

"Don't feel that way in the slightest. I'm saying what I'm saying under no duress. I mean every last word."

I couldn't help but lean in and kiss her. Our lips lingered on one another's in a way that made it obvious that things were about to head back onto the bed unless one of us stopped it. As appealing as the idea of another tumble with Beth sounded, I had other ideas in mind.

I took my lips from hers and sat back. "You have any plans for today?"

"Not really. I planned to come here and give you the news then depending on how our conversation went, either spend the evening crying or celebrating."

I chuckled. "How about a date?"

"A date?"

"A date." I checked my watch, it was a little after six. "It's getting close to dinnertime. How would you feel about making something together and spending the evening in? Something to eat and maybe a little... what do you guys call it, 'Netflix and chill'?"

She let out a loud laugh at that. "I haven't heard anyone say that since probably sometime in 2018, but yeah, that sounds good."

I smiled and kissed her softly on the lips one more time. "Good. Then it's a date."

CHAPTER 17

JACK

The night was wonderful, like something out of a dream.

Beth and I started the evening by putting together a little dinner. I'd been craving a venison roast, and she was more than happy to help with the process. We worked together, cutting veggies and meat and sneaking kisses now and then as we assembled the ingredients, music playing in the background.

We talked while the roast was in the oven— Beth telling me about her family's journey from England to America, and me telling her about my life as a world-traveling accountant.

I glided over the nature of my work and by whom I had been employed. How the hell was I supposed to tell her that I had worked for the damn Mafia? All the same, it didn't feel good to lie by omission. I had to tell her soon, especially since we were about to share a child.

The two hours it took to cook the roast flew by in conversation. I couldn't believe how damn easy it was to talk to her, how just sitting and talking required zero effort at all.

The conversation continued right into dinner, the two of us preparing our plates and sitting down at the kitchen table to continue the discussion and eat.

When dinner was done, we headed into the den for a movie. Once the fire was going, we cuddled together on the couch, Buddy curled up on the carpet near our feet.

Of course, it didn't take long at all before our attention moved away from the movie and on to each other. She tasted like heaven as I kissed her. We moved to the bedroom, spending the next two hours in one another's embrace, making love well into the night.

It had been a perfect evening. Snow began as we held one another, the two of us more than content to spend all the time in the world watching it fall while in each other's arms.

She had to get up early and be home that next morning. We had a quick conversation over coffee on the subject of how and when we were going to drop the bomb on Beau. While we both had the urge to tell him right away, we eventually decided that we ought to take a little time for ourselves to process everything. After all, we weren't just planning a relationship, we were planning the process of raising a damn kid.

We parted that morning with another kiss and an agreement to revisit the issue again soon, deciding how to proceed from there. One more kiss, and she was gone. Buddy and I watched her pull out over last night's dusting of snow and disappear into the woods.

The strangest thing happened after I shut the door... I felt *alone*. I'd lived like I had for years—just Buddy and me —and never once had I experienced the feeling of being alone or the urge to be around people other than my son. I liked the way I lived, wouldn't change a damn thing. But there was something about Beth that made me want to rejoin the world, to see what I'd been missing over the years.

I shut the front door, locking it tight before pouring myself another cup of coffee and starting a fire in the living room. I planned to take a quick trip into town to grab some supplies, get in a little exercise, then nothing but relaxation and reading later. Perfect.

However, a phone call right as I lit the fire snapped me out of my trance.

"Hello?" I stepped away from the fire, putting the phone to my ear.

"Jacky. So good to hear your voice."

And just like that, my morning was ruined.

"Schafer. What do you want?"

"Aw, come on, is that really how you're going to start this conversation? I realize you were always at home working on the books in solitude, but that doesn't mean you can't try to be a little civil."

"Funny as hell listening to a guy like you talk about being civil. I've seen the kind of shit you get up to."

He ignored the dig and kept talking. "Just wanted to check in and let you know that my boys are putting that email together for you now. They're making sure that all the numbers are in order along with everything else. You'll have everything you need to check and make sure the money's clean. And if you spot anything that a certain three-letter organization might find objectionable, all you have to do is flag it so my team here can have it laundered through the proper channels. This'll be the easiest money you make in your life, Jacky. And you can do it all from the comfort of that cabin of yours. Hell, you can do it with that sexy little thing I met at your place yesterday curled up next to you."

I grit my teeth—hard. Part of me wanted to tell Michael to shut his goddamn mouth, to not so much as *mention* Beth. Cooler heads prevailed, however. I knew that giving away how much she meant to me would be a major mistake.

He was trying to get me heated, make me lose my cool. I wasn't about to let that happen.

"I'm going to tell you this one time, and I'm going to give it to you straight, Michael. I'm *not* working for you. It's not happening."

"And why not? You saw the amount of money that's on the table. You'd have to be a damn fool to turn down that kind of payday."

"Then call me a damn fool because it's not happening. I told you when I quit that I was leaving that life for good. And I meant it."

"Here's the deal, Jacky. I'm going to send you the information ASAP. Is the email I have on file still the one you use?"

I opened my mouth, intending to reiterate that I wasn't going to be working for him. But instead, a different idea occurred to me, one that managed to make the corner of my mouth curl in a scheming sort of way.

"Actually, I've got another. I'll text it to you."

"Well then, does that mean you've finally come around, Jacky? That would just warm my cold, black heart if that were the case."

"Just giving you an email. Not saying anything one way or another."

"Fine. Give me the address."

"I'll text it to you," I said again. "After we're done talking, which I hope is now."

"Sure, sure. As long as you're playing ball, I don't need

to waste any more of your time on the phone. It'll be just like old times."

With that, he mercifully hung up.

I wanted to rage, to track Michael down and rip him to shreds for even hinting that he'd do something to Beth. Instead, I calmed myself down and typed a text to him, sending him the email address.

The email I'd given him was one I used for extremely private information; an address encrypted enough that no one but me would be able to get into it. Whatever Michael was planning on sending me would be safe for the time being, giving me a little breathing room to figure out what I was going to do next.

I had too much to lose and couldn't risk getting caught up in illegal bullshit. More importantly, there was no way I'd let any danger come to Beth.

CHAPTER 18

BETH

"Alright, work time's over!" Janie marched into the apartment, pulling me out of my work daze.

"Huh?" I looked up from my laptop, totally oblivious to what time it was. A glance out the window revealed that it was dark, but it'd been dark when I'd started, and there was no way I'd been working for more than a couple of hours.

It hit me. "Holy shit, is it nighttime?"

Janie dropped a white bag of takeout on the counter, the scent letting me know that it was Mexican.

"It's nighttime, and it's taco time, so grab a plate and tell me all about what happened last night. Oh, and as much as I'd love to go sober with you out of pregnant solidarity, it's impossible for me to eat tacos without a Corona."

I laughed. "Come on, I wouldn't dream of telling you to not drink a beer with your tacos on my account."

She flashed me a wicked grin as she headed over to the fridge. "Dig in! Got more than enough for both of us. But the price of tacos is sweet, sweet gossip, so be prepared to pay the price."

By that point, the smell of the tacos had driven me into a frenzy. I opened the big bag, taking out chips, guac, and salsa along with a bunch of individually wrapped tacos. Just as Janie said, there was more than enough for both of us.

I unwrapped one of the tacos as Janie sat down, placing a sugar-free Sprite in front of me and a beer in front of herself.

"First of all, how's work? You're still in the same spot you were when I left, keep in mind, so I'm guessing you got into the zone."

Before answering, I squeezed a lime onto my taco and took a big bite, the meat perfectly tender and seasoned, the tortilla practically melting in my mouth.

"Holy freaking crap, that's good," I said. I couldn't resist. I shoved the rest of the taco into my mouth and chewed, washing it down with a few swigs of Sprite. "I haven't eaten since breakfast, if you can believe it."

"Normally, I wouldn't scold you for something like that, but you're eating for two, remember? You can't be skipping meals like we did in college cramming for finals."

"No, you're right, I'll get better about it. But God, Megan was riding my ass all day today, going over my drawings and telling me to adjust this and tweak that. You just wait, when I send her over the new drawings, I bet she'll freaking change her mind altogether!" I let out a grunt of frustration. "I swear, I'm having trouble figuring out if she's being a standard bridezilla or if she's doing this to torment me."

"Maybe a little of both," Janie said. "But you're still good to go on the wedding, right?"

I sighed, realizing that I was letting the situation get the better of me.

"Yeah. Aside from Megan being a royal pain in the ass,

I'm making progress. She actually signed off on a few of the drawings I sent her a little bit ago. Once we get the décor settled, then I can start putting in orders. After that, I'll work with them on food and invitations and that kind of stuff." The more I talked, the more excited I found myself getting. Megan or not, the day was reminding me of *why* I loved this kind of work to begin with.

"Good," Janie said with a satisfied nod. "Just think, two months from now and you'll be watching this dream wedding unfold, knowing *you* were the one to make it happen and that your career is going to be made once word gets around town."

I had to admit that sounded damn good.

"OK," she said, scooping a chip into the guac and popping it into her mouth. "Wedding talk done. Now, let's hear about your baby daddy who just so happens to also be the groom's daddy. I mean, can you get more complicated than that, B?" She chomped her chip and snapped her finger, sitting back with her beer.

I filled her in, telling her how the drop by turned into an evening date, followed by me staying over. I couldn't help but grin as I spoke, the mere thought of Jack managing to put a smile on my face. When I reached the racy part, I skipped over to our breakfast together.

Janie, of course, wasn't about to let that slide. She threw up her hands, stopping me right in the middle.

"Come on. You had a sexy sleepover with this guy and you're not going to give me *any* details?"

"What? You know I've never been the kiss-and-tell sort of girl."

"That's because you're never doing any kissing to tell about. But now you have, so spill it."

"No way. You want sordid details, go read a romance novel or something."

"Ugh!" She let out a groan of frustration as she stamped her feet. "You have to give me *something*. Like, one detail, at least."

I sighed. "Fine. He's got a lot of hair on his chest."

She raised her eyebrows a bit as if surprised that was the detail I decided to go with.

"Chest hair?"

"Mmm-hmm. It's so hot. Just enough to highlight his chest muscles. And it's a little bit gray, so there's this salt-and-pepper thing going on that's just really sexy."

"OK, I can get down with that. But you're not telling me the little detail that I *really* want to know." Her eyes tracked down between my legs. "How is he... down there?"

I grinned. "Some details, Janie dear, a lady keeps to herself."

∼

One week later Jack and I headed into town to go to my first doctor's appointment. We were in Jack's heavy-duty truck, the engine grumbling powerfully as we drove, the huge size and rugged looks of the truck an amusing contrast to the smaller, sleeker cars in downtown Denver. Buddy was in the back, his paws on the window as he took in the exciting sights.

I was looking out the window too, but not out of excitement. For whatever reason, I was worried. Jack must've sensed this, as he turned down the music and reached over to take my hand.

"You alright over there?" he asked, compassion in his voice.

"Yeah. Sorry, just up in my own head."

"Nothing to apologize for. First doctor appointment's always a little tense. I'm sure you've got a lot on your mind." He gave my hand a squeeze. There was something magical about Jack—his touch and voice was all it took to calm me down.

"It's just hormones. Last night I was cleaning up dinner with my roommate Janie and I started imagining buying tiny little baby socks then started crying out of nowhere."

He laughed. "Sorry, not making fun. Just that it's kind of cute, is all."

"It's cute until I start crying in the middle of work. I feel like I don't have control over my body anymore."

"Well, there's some truth to that. Lots of changes are happening, and in a lot of ways, you're going to feel like you're just along for the ride. But you can get through this, I know it. You're tough as they come."

There was a subtext to what he was telling me, that he'd seen this all before, knew what it was like.

"Thanks. I know this isn't your first rodeo."

He chuckled and gave my hand a squeeze. "You're right. But every pregnancy is a little different even though they are also the same in many ways. I'm no expert, but nothing you've told me is anything out of the ordinary."

I felt a hell of a lot better hearing him say that.

We reached the doctor's office and parked, Jack and I making our way to the door and entering the lobby.

Inside, everything was white and streamlined, clean and modern. Just like with his truck among the sleek cars earlier, Jack looked all sorts of out-of-place in his flannel shirt, shearling jacket, rugged denim and boots. But if he was uncomfortable, he didn't show it in the slightest. Instead, he flashed a warm, charming smile as he approached the receptionist at the front desk.

"Morning," he said. "We've got an appointment for a prenatal exam and… hell, I don't need to do the talking for her."

I laughed at his comment as he stepped aside.

The nurse chuckled along with me. "Welcome! Prenatal with Dr. Monroe?"

"That's right."

"I'll just need your name and some ID, insurance if you have it, and we'll be good to go."

I gave her all of the necessary info, except for my insurance. Jack leaned in and let her know it'd be taken care of on the spot. As much as I hated needing him to pay, I didn't have any other options. Mom and Dad could cover it, but that would mean *telling* Mom and Dad, which I wasn't ready to do just yet. And my business wasn't bringing in nearly enough money that I could fork out the cash for a doctor's appointment.

Jack chatted with the receptionist, making her laugh with one comment or another as he handed over his card. He was confident and charming, which made me appreciate him all the more.

We didn't have to wait long before a nurse called out my name, indicating it was our turn to see the doctor.

"You want me to wait out here?" he asked. "Happy to come with you, but if you want some privacy, I'm absolutely OK with that."

"Not a chance," I replied with a grin.

We reached for one another's hand as we started back. The nurse led us into an examination room where she took my vitals and asked me a few basic questions about the pregnancy and my health in general.

Dr. Monroe strolled into the room soon after. She was tall and skinny with a bob of white hair and eyes that shone with intelligence and warmth in equal measure.

"Well, if it isn't Beth Wheeler!" She grinned as she came over for a hug that I was happy to return. "So good to see you!"

"Same to you, Dr. Monroe."

"My how the time flies; one day you're a teenager coming in for a checkup, the next you're a grown woman coming in with a, ah..." She turned her attention to Jack. "...With a very handsome man for your first prenatal check."

"Pleasure to meet you, Doc," Jack said, offering his hand. "Name's Jack Oliver."

"A pleasure to meet you too, Mr. Oliver."

"Oh, no Mr. Oliver please, Jack will do just fine." He followed this up with another of his irresistible smiles.

"Of course, Jack," Dr. Monroe replied, her tone making it clear that she was already won over by him.

We went over more preliminaries, Dr. Monroe taking notes here and there. It wasn't too long before she set down her clipboard and clapped her hands together.

"Alright! Next step is a quick exam and verifying the pregnancy with a test, then we can do an ultrasound."

Jack raised his eyebrows. "An ultrasound? This early?"

"Well, it sounds like we're a good two and a half months from conception, which means we're getting near the second trimester. So it's actually not that early."

"Yeah, I guess you're right," Jack replied. "I'll give you a little privacy. Come find me when it's time for the ultrasound."

Dr. Monroe didn't waste any time after he left to flick her eyebrows up.

"Now, that's a man who could charm the habit off a nun."

I laughed as I hopped onto the examination table. The test confirmed without a shadow of a doubt that I was pregnant, not that there had been any question. Next step was the ultrasound.

"How're you feeling?" Jack asked as he returned to the room while I was being prepped on the table.

"Good. Nervous and excited all at once."

"Me too," he admitted. He took my hand and squeezed as Dr. Monroe and her assistant set up the machine.

"Should be... right around here..." the tech moved the wand over my belly, the gel cool against my skin. Soon, the *whomp-whomp-whomp* of the baby's heartbeat filled the room, and I let out a squeal of delight. Tears formed in my eyes and I quickly became an emotional mess.

"Sorry," I said. "It's just... I didn't expect to feel so much emotion from that."

"No apology necessary," Jack said with a smile. "You're listening to the most beautiful sound in the world—your baby's heartbeat."

Dr. Monroe didn't react, however, watching as the tech kept moving the wand on my belly. The w*homp-whomp-whomp* of the heartbeat grew faster.

Something was wrong.

"Why does it sound like that?" I asked. "Is everything OK?"

Jack said nothing, a look of mild concern on his face. He was keeping calm as always, but the fact that he hadn't jumped to assuring me nothing was wrong was slightly disconcerting.

"Is something wrong?" I asked again.

Dr. Monroe, who'd been wrapped up in the ultrasound, was quick to offer a smile.

"Sorry, just wanted to make sure."

"Make sure of what?" Jack asked.

"You're not hearing one baby's heartbeat, you're hearing two."

CHAPTER 19

BETH

"Twins?"

Jack and I said the word at the same time, then looked at one another as if we were in a freaking sitcom.

"That's right," Dr. Monroe said, the wand still on my belly. "Sorry for keeping you in suspense, but as you might imagine, this is something you want to make sure of before saying anything." She pointed to the screen. "There. See that fuzzy blob?"

"Uh huh." My heart was racing. I could hardly think straight.

"And see how there's another fuzzy blob right next to it?"

"Sure do," Jack said.

"That's two babies in there. The really fast heartbeat you're hearing is actually two heartbeats. And yes, they both sound healthy. Most importantly, the twins are separated, and there doesn't appear to be any sort of developmental issues. So far, so good."

I stared at the screen, now able to see the two separate babies.

"Do you know what they are?" I asked.

"Little too early for that, unfortunately," Dr. Monroe said. "Not to mention that twins have a bit of a tendency to get in each other's way, blocking the view. Should have better luck at the next ultrasound."

At first, I was a little disappointed that I wouldn't be finding out the gender of my twin babies, but the feeling only lasted for a moment before total happiness overtook me. My hands shot to my belly in excitement.

"Twins!" I said. "I can't believe it!"

"I'm going to grab some info packs and other goodies for you. Be back in a few, OK? Try to think of any questions you might have while I'm gone." Dr. Monroe smiled warmly one more time before heading out of the room and leaving us alone. It became obvious right away that a big reason why she'd left was to give Jack and me a few minutes to process the freaking bombshell that had just been dropped on us.

Jack rubbed a hand over his face and let out a "wow," shaking his head.

"You OK over there?" I asked. He'd been amazing so far, but there was a teensy tiny bit of fear in me that finding out he'd be having not just one baby with me but *two*, would push him over the line.

When he turned back to me, his smile warm and his eyes soft, I realized right away that he was going to be just fine with it.

"Not going to lie, Beth," he said, stepping over and sitting down next to the examination table. "I'm a little terrified."

I laughed. "I can't imagine a guy like you being scared of anything."

"Not scared, that's something different. It's more that,

well, I'm not the young man I was when I had Beau. I'm getting up there."

I took his hand, flashing a sly smile. "Trust me, I know firsthand how much energy you've got."

He laughed. "I suppose you do. But the fact of the matter is I'm ready. I'm ready, and I'm going to do everything I can to make sure those babies are happy and safe."

The tinge of fear I'd felt vanished at his words. "I'll do the same. I promise."

A weird thing happened in those moments, Jack and I sitting next to one another, my hand in his, the image of our two babies frozen on the ultrasound monitor. It was a feeling I'd never felt for a man before.

Was it... love?

I glanced up at Jack, a similar weird look in his eyes. I couldn't help but be certain that he was thinking the same thing. The idea was too much. I pushed it aside, and something else occurred to me.

I sat up, letting my hand slide from his.

"What's up?" he asked.

"I'm going to have to tell my parents about this."

"You think they're going to be upset?"

"I don't know. They've always encouraged me to follow my dreams, be independent, work hard, standard parent stuff. They've never said anything about kids, but I guess they thought about it like I did—that it would happen at some point in the distant future."

Jack nodded. "Beau wasn't planned. His mother and I had talked about kids, but that was something to come far down the line, when both of us were good and established in our careers. I hate to lay the mother of all cliches on you but, well, life has a way of getting in the way of the best-laid plans."

He squeezed my hand, and I smiled. "I'm definitely starting to learn that. So, I want to introduce you to my parents. But something tells me that introducing you to them and then saying, 'hey, I'm pregnant! And oh, by the way, I'm pregnant with *twins!*' Might be a little much for them to process all at once. Maybe we do introductions first, then shortly down the road we can tell them about the babies."

"However you want to handle it works for me, gorgeous. And don't worry—I'll charm the pants off the old man."

I smiled. "I bet you will."

I was nervous, but sitting there with Jack, talking about future plans felt good. It wasn't long before Dr. Monroe returned with a bag of items for me.

"Alright, goodie bag time!" One after another, she pulled out the contents. "We've got info packets, we've got vitamins, we've even got lotion for when that belly of yours starts getting bigger and stretching out."

"Do I need to start taking it easy?" I asked. "I know I'll need to slow down for the twins, but I've got a ton of work to do."

Dr. Monroe's expression turned a bit more serious. "Don't get me wrong your body is going to be going through some major changes, and doubly so for, well, obvious reasons. For now, you should be alright working as usual, though you're going to really need to pay attention to your body and listen to what it tells you. No skipping meals, no missing out on sleep. And when it gets to be too much being on your feet for extended periods, take a rest."

"How soon will I start showing?"

"A little earlier than single pregnancies, but not too much. For a single baby, the timeframe is sixteen to twenty weeks, but for twins you're looking at around twelve to sixteen. With the conception date being so precise, that gives you approximately a couple weeks before you can expect the little ones to start popping out. But keep in mind there's no one-size-fits-all answer with many pregnancy questions. They could end up being tucked in there in such a way you get another month before the baby bump. Best we can do is keep an eye on them. But for now, I say get excited!"

Half an hour later, we were seated in a nearby coffee shop, Jack drinking a cup of the blackest brew I'd ever seen, a decaf latte in my hands.

"Don't put any pressure on yourself to figure this all out right now," he said, his voice deep and clear even in the busy din of the cafe. "Two things to keep in mind—you only need to handle this one day at a time, and we're in this together. I'm here for you, no matter what you need."

He reached over and took my hand, giving it another squeeze. Jack was right. There was a hell of a lot laid out ahead of us, but for now, we had each other. And that made all the difference.

CHAPTER 20

JACK

My mind was so deep in thought that I barely appreciated the view on the way to the lodge. It'd been a few days since the doctor appointment, and aside from texting to make sure she was doing OK and didn't need anything, Beth and I hadn't spoken much to one another.

That was fine. She was staying busy as hell—her way of not getting wrapped up in worry, I was sure. Not to mention that Megan was hardly the easiest client to work for. Beth hadn't told me too much about what was going on, but it was clear from the little bit that she had shared that my future daughter-in-law had her running ragged.

A text from Beau came as I pulled around one of the final bends on the way to the lodge.

You almost here? Megan's getting impatient.

I checked the time, seeing that it was a bit before eleven, which is what we'd agreed upon for the meeting. Beau was no pushover. All the same, I could tell that Megan was placing a tremendous amount of pressure on him, using him as a target for her wedding frustrations.

I pulled over and responded to his text. *Tell her to keep her overpriced shoes on. I'm nearly there.*

I hit send, shaking my head as I dropped the phone into the cupholder and pulled back onto the road. Last thing I wanted was for my boy to have the life drained out of him by some pain in the ass bride. Part of me wondered if I was going to need to have a talk with him about setting boundaries.

Boundaries. I chuckled, shaking my head in disbelief as the word appeared in my mind. The idea of a man like me talking to Beau about boundaries when I'd gone and gotten his ex-girlfriend who was nearly 20 years younger than me pregnant. *Yeah, Jack, your kind of boundaries are real admirable.* Kid would have a good mind to tell me to screw off if I tried to lecture him on that score.

What a mess. While there was no doubt in my mind that it would all end up for the better, getting there was the real issue. Beth and I would have to break the news, and there was no telling how Beau and Megan would take it. I had nightmare images in my mind of Megan firing Beth, trashing her reputation as a wedding planner, and snuffing out her business before it even had a chance to get off the ground.

All those thoughts and more ran through my head as I pulled into the lot. As I scanned the area for a place to park, I spotted Beth. I waved to her and she waved back as I pulled into the spot next to hers.

"Hey!" she called out as I hopped from my truck and onto the dusting of snow on the ground.

"Hey there."

I made my way around the truck, using it as cover to lean in and sneak a kiss. She kissed me right back, and I gave myself a moment to get wrapped up in her scent, her taste, her touch. Thankfully, Beth ended up having some restraint, placing her hands on my chest and gently pushing me away.

"Now, now," she said. "We don't want to start a scandal. Not yet anyway."

I kept my eyes closed for a moment, enjoying the afterglow for just a little while longer. When I opened them, there she was looking just as beautiful as ever, like something out of a dream. Knowing she was carrying my children only made her glow even more.

"Good call," I said with a smile. "Someone's got to be the brains of this operation."

She laughed, the two of us forming up and heading toward the lodge. The place was as bustling as ever—dozens of guests moving about, entering and leaving, some lounging in the lobby, others geared up and going for the slopes.

"So," she said. "Ready for some grub?"

"You kidding? Man like me is always ready to eat."

The plan for the meeting was to try some of the dishes that Beth and Megan had picked out for the reception dinner. Megan had given me strict instructions to not eat breakfast so my taste buds would be good and sharp. Maybe that was a good idea but all I knew for sure was that I was starving.

We stepped into the lobby, the light din of the place inviting. Staff zipped here and there, and most of the sitting areas were occupied by guests sipping drinks or enjoying conversation by the fire. As much as I enjoyed my solitude, I had to admit that I could see the appeal of the place.

Beth and I made our way to the ballroom, chatting and joking around with one another. When we arrived, I held the door for her and the two of us entered.

"There you are!" Beau was at one of the tables near the

entrance, a trio of plates in front of him and one of the lodge's cooks standing at his side. "Food's getting cold!" He smiled as we approached, making it clear he wasn't too bent out of shape.

I stepped in front of the plates, looking them over.

"Uh, let me see here." I put my hands on my hips. "We've got beef, that's easy enough to recognize. And there we've got—"

I didn't get a chance to finish before one of the side doors opened, Megan strolling through. Right away I realized that there was something off about her. Megan always appeared to be composed, maybe even a little tightly wound. However, she never lacked confidence. As I laid eyes on her, I noticed that she seemed frazzled, like there was something weighing heavily on her mind.

"You don't need to guess what the food is, Jack, that's what the chef is for."

I chuckled. "Just having a little fun. How're you, Megan?"

She stopped when she reached the table, flicking her eyes up at me. She didn't hold eye contact, instead glancing away as if she'd seen something she shouldn't have. Then, she did the same sort of quick glance at Beth.

Something weird was going on.

"I'm fine. Let's get to it, okay?"

Beth took over from there. "So, Jack, I'm sure Beau let you know how this is going to go."

I glanced over at Megan one more time. She kept her eyes on the food, not looking up at me.

"He sure did. We've got the three choices the happy couple narrowed it down to for the main course. I'm here to offer my take, maybe break the tie if it comes to that."

"That's right," Beau said. "Maritza's the insanely

talented chef who came up with and prepared the dishes, so she's going to walk us through them."

Maritza, the chef, was petite and pretty with dark hair and caramel-colored skin. She moved with poise and confidence as she approached the dishes.

"For the meals, I went with a few options that are spins on what have been popular with previous weddings here at the lodge. And for Megan, there's a vegan option."

"Uh oh," I said. "Vegan main course might mean that I'll be sneaking in beef jerky."

Beth and Beau laughed, but Megan kept her face straight. I normally would've chalked it up to her not finding my brand of humor to her liking, but it seemed as if there were something else going on. Once more, she was being weird.

Maritza smiled. "Hopefully, it won't come to that. The first dish is something truly classic—beef short rib. It's slow cooked to perfection, served with truffle mashed potatoes, roasted carrots, and a red wine reduction sauce. This has actually been on the menu of our restaurant here at the lodge for decades."

We grabbed our forks and went to work. The short rib was braised perfectly, falling right off the bone as soon as I touched it with the fork. I sampled it along with the veggies, finding the meat delicious, the potatoes and carrots a perfect complement. Megan stuck to the veggies, of course, which meant more meat for me.

"Damn good," I said. "And I'm a man who knows my way around beef."

"I'm a fan," Beau agreed. "Classic, hearty, and a crowd-pleaser."

"Tasty," Beth added.

Megan said nothing, dabbing her mouth and turning her attention to the next dish.

"Second, we have the vegan option. It's a wild mushroom risotto with arborio rice and dairy-free butter."

"What's butter if it's got no dairy in it?" I asked. "Isn't that what makes it butter?"

"*Dad.*" Beau said the word quietly.

"That's a good question, Mr. Oliver," Maritza replied. "This butter is made in-house, with aquafaba, sunflower oil, and emulsifier. It's quite nice, believe it or not."

I flashed her a smile. "Sorry, I'll keep my mouth shut."

Once more, Megan stood aside, her mouth in a flat line. Normally, a comment like that would've gotten a reaction out of her. Not today.

"The risotto is loaded with a variety of locally sourced ingredients, such as shitake, oyster, and portobello mushrooms. For a little color and flavor, the dish is topped with crispy, fried sage leaves and a sprinkle of vegan parmesan. It's a lovely and interesting showcase of some delicious local produce."

We went to it, and I scooped myself a big bite. I'd been skeptical about a vegan option, but damned if it wasn't good and filling and I said so.

"That's so good," Beth said. "So far, that's my winner."

I turned my attention to the last dish—a big slice of meat that looked succulent and delicious.

"Not sure what this is," I said. "But I've got a feeling I'm gonna like it."

"I hope so, Mr. Oliver," Maritza said. "For the last option, I went with another Colorado classic—bison tenderloin. This is a twelve-ounce slice of locally sourced bison, served with parsnips and sweet potatoes and a drizzle of local honey. For a little kick, the dish is finished with a spicy chimichurri sauce with fresh cilantro and parsley."

We took our bites, and right away I knew that was the one for me.

"Damn!" I exclaimed. "Can I get this to go?"

Everyone but Megan laughed.

"So good," Beth said. "Very rustic."

"I like it," Beau added. "A lot. That's my vote right there."

"I don't know about it," Megan said, finally speaking more than a few words. "Isn't it too rich? I don't want people to be in food comas after they eat."

"I get that," Beau said. "But this is really something special. Everyone who comes is going to leave with a little taste of Colorado in their memory."

"They're going to leave with a pound of meat in their gut," she said. "Besides, I can't eat it."

"We'd be happy to prepare the vegan option for you even if you went with the bison for the guests," Maritza offered.

"Well, you wanted my vote," I said. "I say the bison."

"Of course, you would," Megan replied sharply.

"Now what's that supposed to mean?" I asked.

Beau held up his hands, doing his best to stop the discussion. "Listen, babe, I know this is our wedding, and normally I'm fine with letting you make all the decisions. But I'm thinking here we ought to go for something a little more inclusive. Not everyone's vegan, you know.'"

"But this wedding is a reflection of *my* tastes. People are going to leave thinking I'm gobbling red meat for every meal."

"No one's going to think that. Listen, just go with this

one choice of mine and I promise you can choose the rest. This wedding's not just about *you*, remember."

"God forbid I have one thing go how I want!"

"Babe—"

"Don't you *babe* me."

With that, the couple descended into bickering. Beth tried to play peacemaker, holding up her hands and rushing into the mess.

"Why don't you two come with me out onto the balcony."

"Why don't you mind your own damn business, Beth," Megan shot out.

Beth was stunned, her eyes going wide.

It was about all I could stand by and watch.

"Easy, Megan," I spoke. "I don't know what's gotten into you today, but I'm not about to stand here and let you bite the head off of everyone who gives an opinion you don't like."

Megan folded her arms over her chest and scoffed.

"Everyone or just her?" she asked, pointing to Beth. "I mean, she is your girlfriend, isn't she? Or are you just the baby daddy?"

CHAPTER 21

BETH

Oh, shit.
  Oh, shit-shit-shit.
Everyone froze, as if a masked intruder had suddenly burst into the room with a gun in their hands. For a few moments, no one seemed sure what to say or do.

To my surprise, the anger vanished from Megan's face as soon as she said the words. It was replaced with shock, combined with something that looked like... regret? It was hard to say. I wanted to know how the hell she'd known that I was pregnant.

Finally, everyone turned to Beau who stood stunned. I gave a quick nod to Maritza, letting her know there was no need for her to be there. She nodded back, excusing herself as quickly as she could.

"What the fuck is she talking about?"

Jack winced, shaking his head before glancing at me for a quick instant. I wasn't sure how Jack had planned on telling his son what was going on between us, but no doubt that wasn't it.

"Goddamn." Jack turned away, taking a few steps and

running his hand through his thick hair before turning back to Beau.

Beau held up his palms. "OK, someone better tell me what the hell is going on here."

I was still in shock from Megan's outburst, words flying around in my head. I had no idea what to say, how to respond. Thankfully, Jack found his voice and raised his finger to me, giving me a look that said he'd handle it.

"It started a couple of months ago."

"A *couple of months ago?*" Beau asked. "Are you serious?"

"Boy, you wanted to know what happened, I'm going to tell you. But you're going to have to give me the chance to speak." Despite it all, Jack was stern and commanding, his stance firm.

"Fine," Beau said.

Megan stepped back, her arms wrapped around her middle as if protecting herself. The impression I got was that she realized she'd just made a huge mistake that she couldn't take back.

"I was out on Wheeler Hill with Buddy when a saddled horse with no rider ran past..."

From there, he told the story of how he'd found me in the woods unconscious, how he'd brought me back to his place, how he'd nursed me back to health. He explained how we'd gotten caught up in one another, fell for each other on the spot. He glossed over the more intimate details, telling Beau it was only the one night and we didn't see one another again until unexpectedly meeting in the same room we were currently standing in just a couple weeks back.

"We weren't planning on anything to come of it," I added. "It just—"

"It just kind of happened," Beau finished. "So Beth's

pregnant? And you two are what, together? As in, my dad and my ex-girlfriend are having my kid brother or sister *together*?"

"Beau, we were together a long time ago and not for very long. I mean, I never even met your father."

He narrowed his eyes, and I knew right away that I'd made a wrong move.

"It doesn't fucking matter how long ago we dated, it's insane that my dad is fucking my ex, a woman who's nearly half his goddamn age."

He was yelling by the time he was done, his face having turned a shade of red.

"Calm yourself down, son!" Jack projected his voice but wasn't yelling. His volume and tone silenced Beau, who stood with narrowed eyes.

With that, Beau turned and marched out of the room, storming toward the doors leading to the balcony. He pulled one open, stepped out, then slammed it shut.

"Fucking hell," Jack said. He began his own march toward the door that Beau had just gone through. Megan started to follow, but a raise of his finger stopped her in her tracks. "Megan, let me talk to my son alone. You've done enough here today." He didn't even wait for an answer before turning back toward the door and continuing on.

Megan and I were alone. Part of me had expected her to gloat about what she'd done, to have some prissy, pleased-with-herself look on her face as she stood over the chaos she'd created. Instead, she appeared on the verge of tears. Then she said something that I didn't expect at all.

"I'm sorry."

"What?" I wasn't sure I'd heard her correctly.

"I'm sorry. I shouldn't have done that. It… just kind of came out and…"

With that, the waterworks started. She began crying, tears pouring from her eyes. Part of me was cynical about what I was seeing as I stood there stunned. Could it have been some kind of game? Had she said exactly what she'd wanted and now she was escaping blame by turning on the tears?

No, not Megan. Ever since I'd known her she'd never been that kind of girl, never the type to show weakness. She could be a mean girl, sure, but she at least had a spine about it. I'd *never* seen her cry.

"Shit." I stepped over to her, snatching a napkin off a nearby table and handing it to her.

She looked up as I approached, her eyes red.

"Here." I offered the napkin to her, and after a moment of apparently trying to determine if it was a trick or not, she took it.

"Thanks." She wiped her eyes and blew her nose, sobbing a bit more as she did.

"How the hell did you find that out?"

More sobbing, more eye wiping, more nose blowing. Finally, when she was composed, she looked up and spoke.

"It was the other day when you were at Dr. Monroe's. She's my doctor, too."

I just wanted to get in a checkup before all the insanity of the wedding blocked out everything else, you know? Anyway, I was in the bathroom and I came out just in time to see you and Jack leaving, holding each other's hands. I saw the baby swag bag in your hand and it didn't take a genius to figure the rest out."

I thought back to that day, those joyous moments when we walked out of the doctor's office.

I smiled, shaking my head. "We were happy, you know?

I guess we were so wrapped up in the news that neither of us was paying much attention to our surroundings."

"To be fair, I was kind of hiding. I saw you and Jack come around the corner and I ran behind the nearest plant. I know you probably want to kill me right now, but congratulations. You guys did look really happy."

I was still upset, but it did seem like Megan had realized she screwed up and was trying to make amends. I knew staying angry wouldn't help the situation.

I turned my attention to the balcony. Jack and Beau were out there in conversation.

"I hope Beau doesn't throw Jack off the balcony."

Megan laughed, sniffling as she did. "They'll be fine. They're close. They'll work it out. Besides, I don't know if he could lift the old man if he tried."

I laughed, still feeling uncertain about it all. The only thing I could do was hope for the best.

CHAPTER 22

JACK

Beau didn't say a word as I stepped out onto the balcony.

I took a moment to collect myself once the door was shut, to let the cool, fresh March air give me a burst of energy. I needed to gather my thoughts, to make sure I didn't say something stupid that would make the whole thing worse.

When I was ready, I went over to him. Beau stood leaning on the railing, his eyes focused on the horizon, his hands gripping the railing tightly. Didn't take a body language expert to see that he was tense and upset.

Part of me wanted to grill him hard, to find out what he was thinking, what he was feeling. But something I'd learned about Beau early on when he was a kid was that he didn't take kindly to interrogation. The harder I'd come down on him, the more he'd shut down. He was a lot like me in that way.

We stared out onto the valley in silence for what seemed like a long while. A good five minutes passed before Beau finally turned to me and spoke.

"What the hell, Dad?" he asked. "What were you thinking?"

His tone struck me as more confused than angry. I took that as a good sign.

"Son... I know it sounds like a bullshit excuse, but it really did just sort of *happen*. I found her out there unconscious in the cold and brought her inside. All I was planning on doing was making sure she hadn't scrambled her brain from the fall, giving her food and water and sending her on her way. Then the storm hit and..."

"And then one thing led to another."

"Don't know what else I can say. Well, other than the fact that I had not the faintest idea of who this woman was. You dated her in college and never brought her around. How was I supposed to know the two of you had previously dated?"

"So I guess you don't have any pictures of me around the place. I never thought to look any time I was over."

"Oh, I've got a couple. Keep 'em in the bathroom."

I gave him a small smile after I spoke. He responded with a weak one of his own, another good sign.

"It was dark," I said. "She was on the couch by the fire."

"Didn't want her to see that ugly mug of yours?"

That got a laugh out of me. "You got me. Look, kid, things happened and I thought that'd be the end of it."

A few beats of silence fell, the wind kicking up in the distance and bending the tops of the pines in the valley.

"Shit, I can't believe what kind of a man-whore my dad ended up becoming."

Another laugh. "Believe it or not, living the kind of life I do doesn't exactly leave a lot of opportunity to be a man-whore."

He smiled, then turned his attention back to the valley,

clearly something else on his mind. After a moment or two, he spoke.

"You care about her?"

"Of course, I do. She's a damn fine woman. And she's pregnant."

"That's not what I asked. I asked if you have feelings for her."

"I feel... something. There's no damn doubt in my mind that I could fall for her. But hell, we sure did this thing backwards, didn't we? I want to try dating her, see if I can get to know her better."

"I want to be mad about this, Dad, and a good part of me is. But at the same time, I've never seen you like this about a woman before. Trust me, I've spent a hell of a lot of time wondering if you were ever going to find someone."

"I've wondered that too, Beau. I loved your mother like no other and never thought I'd even want to be with someone again, but Beth surprised me. Whatever happens, kid, I hope you're OK with it. Beth's having our baby, and that means she's going to be a part of our lives for the rest of our lives." I caught myself as I spoke. "Shit. Babies."

At the word, Beau finally turned toward me. "Did you say *babies*?"

"I did. She's having twins."

"No way." He shook his head in total disbelief. "*Twins*?" He laughed. "Dad, those kids are gonna eat you alive. Hell, they're going to come out being like 'oh, grandpa's here. But where's Dad'?"

A true belly laugh escaped me and I felt a huge amount of relief. If he was joking around, that meant he was on the way to forgiving me. I decided to push my luck.

"Come here, kid." I clapped my hand onto his shoulder and he turned around, the two of us stepping into a big hug.

"Let's get back in there," he said when we parted. "Got a big conversation ahead of us."

"No kidding."

∾

A few days later, I was on the phone with Beth. I figured it was time to connect to the wider world, so I'd signed up for satellite internet, which was a hell of a lot more reliable than what I'd had before.

"Does this mean you're going to get a smartphone next?" Beth asked.

"Not a chance in hell. I like my flip phone, thank you very much."

She laughed. "I bet you anything you'll go back on that. Have you seen the cameras on smartphones these days? Are you really telling me that you're not going to want as many pictures of the twins as possible?"

"Believe it or not, there was a time when people lived their lives without taking pictures of every little thing, cute babies or not."

"Right, that time was called the bronze age, when you were born."

I laughed and she did, too. "You know, you've got such a sexy phone voice that I don't even mind if you're using it to poke fun at my age."

"Good. Because I'm going to be doing it a lot."

More laughs.

"On a serious note," I said. "I'm looking forward to seeing you again."

"Same here. I've been so wrapped up in Beau and Megan's wedding stuff that I haven't had a chance to go out anywhere."

"So, Megan stayed true to her word and kept you on board?"

"Sure did. It wasn't like she had much of a choice—not a chance in hell she'd find someone to replace me at this stage in the game."

"Well, you're doing a damn good job so far."

"Thanks."

"How about tonight?"

"What about tonight?"

I chuckled, realizing I lost her. "Seeing one another. Too soon?"

"Not at all. But well, I don't have anything to wear." Her voice took on a playful tone.

"What're you wearing right now?"

"Over or under my clothes?"

My cock twitched to life at the thought of Beth in her underwear.

"Let's start with over."

"Sweater and jeans."

"Just how I like you. Wear that."

"I think I can handle that."

"Now, how about under?"

She chuckled. "You'll have to wait and find out. That is, if you're a good boy."

"I'll be on my best behavior."

Right after I spoke, Buddy barked outside. I stepped over to the window, watching as a sleek, dark blue sedan pulled onto the property.

"Listen, gotta go. Someone's here."

"Someone's there?"

I didn't like lying to her, but the last thing I wanted was to pull her into the part of my old life that I was trying to keep hidden.

"Neighbor buying some firewood."

"Oh, OK."

"Six tonight work?"

"Sure. I'll text you my address."

"Sounds good. See you then."

I hung up and slipped the phone into my back pocket, keeping my eyes on the car. The door opened and it wasn't Michael who stepped out, but a woman. She was tall and trim, her hair a deep red and shoulder length. Her face was slender and pretty, her outfit a professional dark gray pantsuit with a black trench coat over top of it. It was hard to pin down her age, but I guessed late twenties, early thirties. She looked over the cabin as she approached, Buddy watching her with careful eyes.

I opened the door. She pulled off her sunglasses, revealing a pair of dark brown eyes.

"Jack Oliver?" she asked.

"That's me. Want to tell me who you are and what you're doing on my property?"

She wasted no time reaching into the inner pocket of her trench coat and flashing me a badge.

"Agent Amy Miller—FBI."

Shit.

"I want to talk to you about Michael Schafer."

She approached, her face an expression of pure professionalism. Agent Miller wasn't there to screw around. I could only hope that my past hadn't caught up with me in a way I wouldn't be able to escape.

CHAPTER 23

BETH

I was *so* ready to see Jack again. I had a little secret, though—I wasn't wearing what we'd agreed upon. I was sure he'd like what I had in store for him, however.

Lively music played from my phone, an African pop Spotify playlist that I always put on whenever I was in a high-energy mood. I danced and sang to the music, even though I didn't know the words.

I was enjoying getting the evening ready. Pad Thai was warming in the wok and delicious smells filled up the place. I'd sent Janie packing for the night, which actually worked out well since she'd been meaning to visit her parents anyway.

My phone buzzed a few minutes before six. It was a text from Jack letting me know he had arrived. I replied, telling him to get his butt up to my door. Just the thought of him coming to visit was enough to make me tingle down below. If I had been wearing panties, I was sure the mere thought of opening the door and seeing him there would've been enough to soak them.

But I wasn't wearing panties.

I plated the food, pouring a couple glasses of non-alcoholic sparkling cider in preparation for his arrival. It didn't take long at all before a heavy *thunk-thunk-thunk* sounded at the front door. I turned down the volume of the music a bit.

"Coming!"

This evening goes the way I want, I sure will be.

I laughed to myself at my silly joke before stepping in front of the mirror in the hallway. I was in nothing but a silk floral-patterned robe, the length short enough to show off most of my legs. I wore no bra underneath, of course, the neckline of the robe pulled open to show off the span of my upper body from in between my boobs all the way down to my belly button. I couldn't help but grin at the sight of myself.

When I was ready, I hurried over to the door, opening it slowly. I leaned against the nearby shelf, posing in such a way that would make it abundantly clear what I had in mind.

"Good evening, Mr. Oli—"

Suddenly, the shelf gave way and I started to fall. Just then a huge arm shot out, catching me before I did.

"You OK, gorgeous?" I heard Jack ask in his deep and sexy as hell voice.

"I think so," I answered with a somewhat embarrassed laugh.

Jack effortlessly helped me to where I was once again steady on my feet, holding on to me as if I weighed nothing at all. I blinked hard as he stood before me, a knowing smirk on his face.

"You nearly took a hell of a tumble there," he said.

"Gotta be a little more careful, you're walking for three now." He gently nudged me away so he could enter then closed the door.

My heart was already racing from the near fall. The sight of Jack in front of me made it beat even faster, so hard I felt a touch dizzy. He looked so handsome it was ridiculous. He was wearing jeans, a flannel and boots, but a more dressed-up version of his typical ensemble. His jeans were dark, his flannel tucked in, and his boots actually polished.

"You look nice," I said, giving him a once-over.

He chuckled, glancing at his outfit. "You like this? Figured I'd wear something that wasn't covered in dirt and dog drool. We're having a date, after all."

"Well, I kind of had a surprise for you," I said. "I was thinking we might... you know, stay in."

With that, I licked my lips and cocked my hips to the side, flicking my eyebrows up. I was doing my best attempt at sexy.

He laughed, stepping close to me and putting his hands on my hips. "You're a good wedding planner, you know?"

I cocked my head to the side in confusion. "I like to think so."

"Right. In fact, I think you're so good at it that I'm going to recommend you not quit your day job."

I laughed, realizing what he was saying. "What, you weren't totally wrapped up in the sensual spell of seduction that I cast on you from the moment I opened the door?"

He wrapped his arms around me, pressing his body against mine. "Is that what that move was? Casting a spell?"

I felt the heat from his body, felt his cock stiffen against me.

"Something like that. And judging by what I'm feeling against my leg, I'd say it worked."

"Let me show you how well."

I closed my eyes and smiled, knowing that a kiss was coming. Sure enough, his lips met mine, his hands reaching into my robe and falling onto my hips, his touch warm and rough in that now-familiar way. I kissed him back, my own hands falling onto his jacket.

"Now, this isn't fair," I said, breaking the kiss for long enough to speak. "I'm practically naked and you're still completely dressed."

"You're right," he said in between kisses along my neck. "I seem to have you at a disadvantage."

Jack took my words to heart, slipping off his jacket and tossing it aside. I worked the buttons of his shirt, pulling it out of his pants and moving it over his shoulders. With a little teamwork, we soon had him down to nothing but his boxer briefs, the two of us moving slowly to the bedroom.

We kissed harder, Jack reaching under my robe and sweeping his hands over my legs and up to my ass. He lifted me off the ground, a squeal of surprise shooting from my mouth. He carried me over to the bed, setting me down on the edge and dropping down to his knees. He covered my inner thighs in kisses, tingles spreading through my body, the tickling of his beard against my skin bringing a smile to my face.

I moaned languidly when he finally brought that gorgeous mouth of his to my center, parting my lips gently and teasing my clit with his tongue. I gasped, running my hand through his thick hair.

"Crazy how every bit of you tastes like heaven," he said, glancing up at me with a sly grin on his face. "You're something else, you know that?"

His words sent a flutter through my heart, moans pouring from my mouth as he returned to licking me. It was hard to focus, the sensations so intense, but through it all I managed to steal a few peeks of the sight of him between my legs, one huge hand on my thigh, the fingers of the other holding me open as his tongue moved over my clit.

"Just like that," I sighed. "Just like that."

He alternated his movements, first making slow circles with the tip of his tongue, then pressing it firmly and flat against me, then doing it all over again. Jack moved one finger inside, the pleasure building and building until I couldn't take it anymore. My breathing quickened, shrieks of pleasure sounding.

When he sensed that I was getting close to release, he glanced up at me with that same smirk on his lips.

"Now, you remember my rule, right gorgeous?"

"Mmm-hmm." I nodded quickly, barely able to focus on anything but the overwhelming pleasure building and building within.

"I want to hear it." His finger moved in and out of me, the sensation of it only making me want more of him.

"No coming until you say so."

"Good girl."

He returned to licking and caressing and pumping me with his finger. Jack brought me to the edge of total release. But I obeyed his command, not allowing myself to go over the line. I glanced down to see him flick his eyes up at me, his gaze narrowed in such a way that made it obvious he knew exactly how he was making me feel.

I squirmed and writhed, my hands on the back of his head. Finally, right when I reached the point where I couldn't take anymore, he spoke.

"Now."

The pleasure released, crashing and exploding all

throughout my body. I let out a scream, my thighs shaking as he continued to eat me out. The orgasm receded, and Jack sat up, wiping my arousal from his mouth with the back of his hand.

"OK," I said, grinning mischievously. "My turn."

CHAPTER 24

JACK

I loved that naughty twinkle in her eye. Beth put her hands on my legs, moving me over to the bed where I'd just made her come moments before. I was stiff and solid as a steel beam, feeling on the verge of tearing through my shorts.

"Kind of unfair that you got to taste me, but I haven't done the same," she said, seductively sliding her hands over my thighs all the way to the waistband of my underwear. She slipped her fingertips underneath and slowly pulled them down, first exposing the coarse hair below my belly and the base of my cock.

"I'm big on fairness," I replied with a grin. "Especially in the bedroom."

"Same here. So glad we could come to a diplomatic solution."

"That's right. I'd hate for things to get too heated."

She pulled my underwear further down , enough for my cock to spring out of its fabric prison. Beth smiled, licking her lips as she laid eyes on it, as if she couldn't imagine anything more delicious. She placed her hand on the base of my cock, wrapping her slender fingers around it and stroking me slowly.

"That feel good?" she asked.

"So damn good. But I bet you can make it feel even better."

"I'm more than up to the challenge."

With that, she leaned in close and placed her lips on my head, then moved along my length until she reached my balls. After a bit more licking, she went right back up to my head.

I groaned with pleasure, watching with eager, hungry eyes as she opened her mouth and enveloped the head of my prick. She sealed her lips around it, lashing it with her tongue as she kept her eyes on me, her hand cradling my balls and squeezing them softly.

The sight was about the sexiest damn thing I'd ever seen. I kept my eyes on her as she descended, taking more of me into her mouth until she reached about halfway, where she couldn't fit any more.

She moved up slowly, letting me fall out of her mouth so she could lavish me with licks and kisses, then going back down. She built up a steady rhythm, moving up and down, soft, wet sounds filling the air. It didn't take much before I could feel an orgasm rising up from the base of my cock. I swept her hair away, eager for a full view of her at work.

I could sense the point of no return approaching. I placed my hand under her chin and carefully guided her off. She flicked her tongue against the tip of my cock once more as she sat back up.

"I'd be more than happy to finish you," she said.

I grinned. "As much as I'd love to watch that, I'm not even close to done with you yet."

I reached down, guiding Beth to her feet and stood up

with her. We kissed hard and deep, animal passion behind each press of my lips against hers, each flick of our tongues against one anothers. When I was ready, I wrapped my arm around the small of her back, opening her robe with the other. Her breasts and stomach and curves were so tantalizing that I could hardly think straight. And knowing she was carrying our babies only made me want to treat her more tenderly.

With a smooth, careful motion, I laid her onto her back. I wasted no time climbing on top of her, grabbing my cock by the base and guiding it to her opening. She placed her hands on my ass and pulled me down, my cock parting her lips and driving inside.

"Goddamn, you feel like heaven." It was the truth, through and through. Her walls were warm and velvety, gripping me tightly as I pushed deep inside.

I began to move inside of her, in and out, one arm propping me up and the other wrapped around her. I held her close, the two of us forming a perfect pace, flowing together as if our bodies were one. It didn't take long before I was ready. I leaned down and whispered the command to come in her ear and she obeyed as always. We held one another close as we came in unison, kissing deep, our cries of pleasure muffled by one another's lips.

I stayed inside her for a time, Beth resting her head on my shoulder. When I pulled out, I rolled to her side and held her close against me. A gentle snowfall began outside, soft flutters of white dancing against the window. But her eyes were what I really couldn't take my eyes off of. We gazed at one another, and three little words formed in my mind that I couldn't help but utter out loud.

"I love you."

Her face stayed flat at first, and for a moment I worried I

might've said something she wasn't prepared to hear. When a smile spread across her face, however, I knew she felt the same way.

"I love you, too."

The words filled me with a happiness I could hardly wrap my head—or heart—around. I reached my hand down, placing it on her belly.

"I promise to take care of all three of you for the rest of my life. I swear it."

She answered my statement with a tender kiss that I happily returned.

CHAPTER 25

BETH

It was a month out from the wedding, and as I zipped along the sidewalks of downtown Denver, trying to maneuver through the tight knots of people and not graze them with my burgeoning baby bump, I was feeling the stress.

The last month had gone well, all things considered. Beau and Jack had patched things up, and Megan had been shockingly easy to deal with. As much of a princess as she could be about the planning, her going over the line and blurting out our secrets seemed to have chastened her a bit.

That was fine with me. She'd toned down her demanding nature, and actually became somewhat of a helpful partner in getting things organized. We weren't exactly best buds, but our relationship had mellowed to where the planning was actually becoming fun again.

I had two stops on my agenda. The first was to the florist that Megan had picked out, where she'd finally selected the arrangements she wanted for the tables. That part would be easy. The next, on the other hand, tied my stomach in knots just to think about—I was taking Jack to meet my parents for the first time.

Even though I had told Jack I wanted him to meet them first and then tell them about the babies, my quickly expanding waistline had made that nearly impossible. A week prior, I'd gone over to their house for dinner and had shared the news. They were shocked at first, but the shock quickly turned to excitement at the prospect of being grandparents.

Of course, when the excitement subsided, the question of who the father was came up. There was no point in sugarcoating it, of trying to lie by omission or anything like that. So, I gave them the straight-up answer—the father was a man named Jack, he happened to be my ex's dad, and he was nearly twice my age.

Those little details had taken a little more time to go down smoothly. First, Mom and Dad had to walk through the answer, figuring out just how Jack and I had met, how he figured into the wedding I'd been planning. I had to reassure them all the while, letting them know that Jack wasn't some half-feral man who lived in a cave. Thankfully, Mom having already seen his place when she'd picked me up the day after Jack and I had met helped make my case.

Still, I was nervous for them all to meet. I stepped into the florist, scents of fresh flowers surrounding me. I let my eyes linger on the roses, a smile forming on my lips. Red roses could be a little cliché, but all the same a huge bouquet of them filled me with excitement like nothing else.

"Morning!" the florist called out as I weaved my way through the aisles. "Something I can help you with?"

"Sure is. I'm planning the Oliver-Goodjohn wedding."

The woman's eyes lit up as soon as I said the name of the couple. "Perfect timing! I just finished the sample centerpiece."

"Oh, that's awesome! The bride said she already decided, so I'm just here to confirm and put in the order."

"Sure, sure. Let me grab it. Be right with you."

I watched as she turned around to the glass cases of flowers behind her. There were quite a few huge, gorgeous arrangements behind the glass, and with a smile on my face I expected the florist to grab the biggest one.

To my surprise, she grabbed the smallest.

"Here it is!"

I stepped over to the counter and took in the sight of the floral centerpiece. It was gorgeous, for sure, but... modest.

"This is the Oliver-Goodjohn wedding centerpiece?"

The florist regarded me with an expression of concern. "Not to your liking?"

"No-no-no, that's not it at all. I love it, in fact." I wasn't lying—the arrangement was stunning with yellow, purple and white the dominant colors. "Just that... the bride has, well, exacting and expensive tastes. I was half-expecting you to haul it out with a wheelbarrow."

She laughed. "Nope. When I spoke to Miss Goodjohn she was quite sure of what she wanted, something modest but beautiful, with a fresh, spring vibe, as she called it. So, I went with some hyacinths, along with lovely little sweet peas, and some peonies for color. And of course, some blush roses in the center."

"Hey, I'm into it. Let me just double-check with the bride and we'll be good to go."

"Of course."

I snapped a picture and sent it to Megan, the response coming a second later.

That's perfect! Put in the order! A few heart emojis followed.

For a second, I found myself wondering if Megan had been replaced by an alien clone or something. But her words were on my screen, clear as day. I heart-reacted and slipped my phone back into my purse.

"She loves it! Let's get the order started."

The florist and I spent a few minutes going over the finer points of the contract, and once it was settled and signed, I was on my way, totally pleased to have knocked out one more difficult part of the planning.

With that taken care of, I allowed myself a little bit of mental space to enjoy the walk. I had the meeting with Mom and Dad to worry about, but in the meantime, I could at least enjoy the sun and the fact that it was the first day in a while that hadn't been insanely cold. It was almost starting to feel like spring was just around the corner.

I had a little time to kill before I was due at the coffee shop, so I decided to head over to Civic Center Park and get some steps in. The twins were starting to show, and I had a good feeling it wouldn't be long before even something as simple as a walk in the park would become, well, *not* a walk in the park.

Just as I crossed the street, however, a voice called out to me.

"Hey, Beth!"

I froze. The voice certainly didn't belong to Jack. The older man's voice didn't sound familiar at all. My first instinct was to start moving in the opposite direction as quickly as possible.

But instead, I turned around and was greeted with the sight of the man I had seen at Jack's place a few weeks back. He was dressed in a sharp suit, gold rings on his fingers, designer sunglasses on his face. His style was rich with a hint of gaudiness. I didn't care for the man when I first met him at Jack's and the feeling was even more intense the second time.

"There you are," he said as he approached and came to a stop. "Been looking all over for you."

He grinned as he drew closer, and it made me nervous as hell.

"I'm sorry." I said. "I have no idea who you are."

My fight-or-flight was kicking in, and I glanced around to make sure there were a few people close by if I needed help. It was then that I spotted an expensive-looking black luxury car pulled up to the curb just a little bit behind the man. The back windows were tinted pitch-black but I could see the driver, his eyes on both of us.

"Oh, where are my manners?" he asked. "I almost forgot that we weren't formally introduced the last time we met." His demeanor was odd. He was over-friendly and overconfident. Both were off-putting.

He offered me his hand. "My name's Michael Schafer. I'm an old colleague of Jack's from back in the day. As a matter of fact, he used to work for me."

I ignored his outstretched hand and he lowered it without seeming bothered by the rebuke. I knew I needed to get away.

"I don't want to keep you. I'd never dream of wasting the time of a busy woman like yourself, pregnant with twins and working at the same time. Impressive, really."

That reveal of personal information was all I needed to hear.

"I don't know what you want, but I'm leaving."

I started to turn. Before I could, Michael's hand shot out with surprising speed and grabbed my upper arm, holding me in place. I wanted to scream, but I was too shocked to say or do anything. He leaned in, flashing me a sinister smile.

"I've got a message for you, beautiful, that I want you to pass along to our good friend Jack. Tell him that he's been a very, *very* bad boy, ignoring my calls and texts. Tell him that I'm not a man who takes kindly to being ignored, and if he doesn't get with the program, I'll have to stop by his cute little cabin in the woods and visit him in person—maybe while his pregnant girlfriend is there."

I came to my senses suddenly, yanking my arm away and shooting him a hard look.

"This is your first and only warning, asshole—get the hell away from me." I was scared, but not scared enough to not stand up for myself.

I didn't wait to hear his response, turning and hurrying down the sidewalk as quickly as I could. To my surprise, he didn't call out after me. Instead, he let out a loud laugh, as if my threat had been nothing more than an amusement to him.

It wasn't until I was near the end of the block before he spoke again.

"You'd better have that talk with Jacky, pretty girl! Otherwise, there might be some complications in your future!"

His threat made my blood run cold. I hurried, moving as quickly as I safely could, only turning and glancing over my shoulder to make sure he wasn't running after me. It didn't take long before I spotted the coffee shop, the sight of Jack seated near the window about the sweetest relief I could imagine. I burst through the door, tears in my eyes as I hurried over to him.

He stood, clearly confused and concerned.

"You alright, gorgeous?"

Without saying a word, I threw myself into his arms, crying silent tears against the warmth of his coat.

CHAPTER 26

JACK

I knew something was wrong from the moment I laid eyes on her. And when the tears began to flow, fear gripped my heart. My first worry was that something had happened to the twins.

"Easy, darlin'," I said. "Come over and sit down. Tell me what's wrong."

She wiped her eyes, shaking her head.

I reached over and took her hand. "Is there something wrong with the babies?"

Her eyes flashed. "No. No, they're fine."

Relief like nothing I'd ever known washed over me.

"Good. That's good to hear. Now, tell me what happened. What's got you so shaken up?"

Beth nodded before lifting the glass of water I handed her and taking a slow sip, giving herself a few more moments to compose.

She told me the whole sordid story, how Michael Schafer, that miserable, weaselly prick, ambushed her out of nowhere and threatened not only her, but the lives of our babies. However intense the relief I'd felt knowing the babies were fine had been, the anger that ran through me after Beth told me what Michael had done was a hundred times more intense. I wanted to rip the fucker apart, limb from limb.

I kept calm, not wanting to add any more stress onto the load Beth was already carrying.

When she finished telling me what had happened, she wiped her eyes one more time, her expression turning grave.

"Jack, I know you mean it when you say you're going to protect me and make sure nothing happens to me and our babies. But I need to be able to trust you, and there's no way that's going to be possible if there's one of those huge, black redacted bars over twenty years of your life."

"Eleven years."

"Huh?"

"Not twenty. Eleven." I took a sip of my coffee, looking out of the window at the crowds passing by. I had to give myself some time to think about where to begin, how to start. Never in my life had I sat down and shared the story of my time working for Michael Schafer. I'd hoped I never would.

"Back when I was in my twenties, about your age, I believe, I was having a hard time. Charlotte was gone and I was raising Beau all alone, and while I was making decent money working as a freelance accountant here and there, it wasn't enough."

I allowed myself a wry chuckle at my own words. "Actually, that was wrong. It was enough, just not *fast* enough. After losing my wife, I vowed that I'd do whatever it took to make sure that Beau had whatever he needed, that he'd never want for a damn thing. I was working for clients, socking away a little money, building a cushion for our future. But it wasn't *fast* enough.

"I was good at what I did; knew my way around an adding machine, you could say. My reputation started to get around, and not just in the law-abiding world. I was at a bar one night, Charlotte's parents looking after Beau. I was going over my income, wondering how the hell I was going to provide Beau with the life I knew he deserved. That's when Michael Schafer approached me."

I went on. "He came up to me, all his gold and fancy suits and big grins. Told me he'd heard about me from a friend of a friend, said that I was just the man he'd been searching for to help out with his organization. He told me he wanted to hire me on retainer, do some off the books numbers for him and his associates. Even then, stupid kid that I was, I knew something was up. But man, when he stuck that little stack of hundreds in my hand as payment for my time and as encouragement to think it over, I was sold."

I shook my head in disbelief, Beth's eyes locked on me.

"I was just a stupid kid, a single dad with a baby to raise. So, I went for it. Michael was smart, leading me in with work that seemed pretty damn innocuous. Three times a week he'd send a car for me, one that would take me to an office outside of town. There, I'd work on some books, have a guy review them, then leave with a fat cash payment. I had no idea what kind of work I was doing—far as I could tell, I was doing nothing more than balancing the books for a few businesses around town. Deep down I knew something was off, but for the most part, it seemed legit.

"And man was I making money. Made more in a few months than I'd made in the last couple of years. I bought a new house for me and Beau, new car, new clothes. I wasn't even thirty and I was already feeling like king shit. But things were getting stranger with the work. I came to realize that I wasn't just balancing books, I was *cooking* them. Michael would come in with books of numbers that looked all kinds of wrong, told me to make them look right. No way to do that without skirting the law.

"But I did it. Stupid me, I did it. I know what I told myself at the time, that sure, I was cooking books. But I wasn't the one *running* these businesses, you know? That all changed one day. I was in the middle of my work when I heard a muffled scream from down the hall. Should've just ignored it, kept my head down. But remember what I said about being a stupid kid?"

I shook my head again. Beth continued to watch me in silence, concern on her face.

"I followed the noise and spotted some guy being dragged into a room. I peeked around the corner to see this poor SOB getting tied to a chair, Michael and a couple of other goons working him over, beating the shit out of him, asking him about some money. I was smart enough to realize that I was seeing something I most definitely shouldn't have, but it was too late. Michael spotted me, flashing me this horrible grin as if he had me right where he wanted me."

"What happened?"

"He met me in the office later, said that it was time I knew what kind of business I was working for. Took me out to this club downtown, a place where there were women and drugs and gambling and every other vice someone could want. Had me meet the men in charge. Turns out they already knew who I was from my work."

"Did you do any of that stuff? The drugs, the women..."

I shook my head vehemently. "No. Never been a gambler, and I've always been way too serious about staying in shape to mess around with anything other than my whiskey. And women... never cared about any of them, too damn busy worrying about my boy and grieving my wife."

She seemed relieved, a held breath escaping her.

"Anyway, from there I was part of the life. I worked for Michael, who provided me with a solid income. He kept me out of the dirty parts of mob life, though he'd made it clear the offer was on the table if I ever wanted to move up in the ranks. The answer to that was always a *hell no*. I was making good money, but working for those kinds of men meant I, and more importantly, Beau, were always in danger. So, I worked and I invested. Little by little, my investing started paying off. After a decade or so, I was making more off my investments than I was working for Michael."

"That's when you quit."

"Yep. Beau was getting ready to start high school, and I wanted a clean break. Told Michael that I was done, that after the end of the year, I was moving on. I was... surprised at how easily he let me go. At the time, I thought it was because he was happy to not have to pay me the small yearly fortune he had been to keep me on board. Looking back it was obvious that he'd never truly intended to let me go."

One more sip of coffee. "Enough time had gone by that I'd gotten a little cocky, thinking that maybe he really and truly had let me go. But when I saw him step out of that car, I knew that my old life had caught up with me."

She looked away, taking a long moment to process.

"This is a lot, Jack. I had a strong suspicion that there was something you were hiding from me, but I didn't think it was the *mob*." She spoke the last word in a hush, making sure that no one was nearby and listening in.

"I know, I know. But damn, it's the kind of thing that

there's no good time to bring up. And foolish as it might've been, part of me was hoping it'd just go away. No luck there, I suppose."

She nodded, determination on her face. "OK. Well, we need to figure out what to do now."

"Got a contact in the FBI," I said. "Spoke with her about trying to set him up. But in the meantime, God, I know this is sudden, but I'm thinking it's the best call to have you move in with me, Beth. I can keep you safe out there, and it'd be a load off my mind."

"I don't know. I need to think about it more."

"Understood. Just know that the offer's on the table."

She reached over and squeezed my hand. As we sat in silence, the front door to the café opened, a middle-aged couple entering that I had no doubt were Beth's parents.

"Time for a gear shift," I said, nodding toward the entrance. "Think they'll like me?"

"I bet you they will. Come on. Let's go say hi."

We rose, and hand-in-hand, we went over.

Life was getting more complicated by the moment. All I could hope for was that it wouldn't pull me—and the woman I loved—under.

CHAPTER 27

JACK

"Shots, shots, shots... *woo hoo!*"

I was in the middle of one of the most important phone calls of my life, and all I could hear was the commotion of the boys at Beau's bachelor party. We were all in the penthouse of a luxury hotel downtown, yours truly footing the bill. Didn't mind that one bit—Beau deserved to have a nice night, and them getting hammered in a hotel room meant they weren't causing trouble around town.

The view from the penthouse balcony was amazing, a sweeping panoramic of Denver at night. I loved my life out in nature, but views like that made me understand the appeal of cities.

"You alright over there?" Agent Amy Miller's voice came through loud and clear.

I sipped my whiskey. We'd just returned from dinner out not too long ago, Beau and the crew wasting no time getting into their cups.

"Just babysitting a group of unruly kids," I said, a small smile on my face. "Son's bachelor party."

She chuckled. "And you're spending the party talking to an FBI agent. You sure know how to cut loose, Jack."

That got a laugh out of me. "Yeah well, life has a way of sneaking up on you. And so does a hangover over forty."

"You OK having this conversation now?" she asked. "We can wait. But not too long, though."

"Yep, now's good. I'm out on the balcony. Only reason I can hear them is because they're carrying on like a pack of wild animals."

"OK. Just want to make sure you're good with every step before we take it."

"Sure am. Wouldn't be talking to you if I weren't. And I'm making this call on a burner phone, just like you asked."

"Understood." While Agent Miller had something of a light side to her, she was mostly all business. I liked that; it meant she was serious about putting that prick Schafer behind bars. "Anyway, fill me in. You said he talked with Beth?"

"He sure did. Accosted her in the middle of the goddamn street downtown." I went into it, giving her the rundown of what had happened.

"OK, if he's pulling stunts like that in broad daylight, it means that he's getting desperate."

"That's what I figured."

"Then we need to take him down before he does anything crazy. First of all, I'm going to need those emails."

"Not gonna work. Schafer's a thug, but he's not stupid. I've looked over the emails, and there's nothing in them connecting him to any crime."

"That's what I was afraid of. Anyway, if we're going to put him away, we're going to need *some* kind of evidence. If the emails won't work, then that means we're going to need a wire."

I winced. "Yeah. That's what I figured."

"I know it's not ideal. I've worked with enough witnesses to know that even when recording someone who really needs to get put behind bars, lies and deceit aren't fun."

"Yep. Never been the underhanded sort."

"And I get that; I really do. But the fact of the matter is that it's our only chance if we're going to lock his ass up. I don't want to put too fine a point on it, but you and Beth aren't going to be safe until he's in jail. Scum like Schafer will do whatever they need to, threaten whoever they need to, in order to get what they want."

"I know the man. You're preaching to the choir here."

"In that case, we'll need to set up a meeting. Don't worry—the wires that people wear nowadays aren't those clunky, tape-recorder things from 80's cop movies. The ones we have today are very small, so tiny that they're hard to find even with a pat down."

"That's no small consolation. Alright, Agent Miller, I'll get in touch with Michael and keep you posted."

"Good. And thanks again, Jack, you're doing the right thing."

I hung up, slipping the clunky burner phone into my pocket next to my clunky regular phone. The call over, I stared out at the city, wondering what the future might hold. The wedding was just a short time away, and I hated that I had this Schafer bullshit to worry about, preventing me from being able to enjoy my own damn son getting married.

I sipped my whiskey, my mind going from Beth to the twins to the wedding to Beau to Schafer and all the way back again. It was damn hard to believe that just a few short months ago all I had to worry about was chopping firewood for the winter and making sure Buddy had grub to eat.

"Yo, Dad?"

Beau's voice snapped me out of my trance. I turned to see my son standing at the open door to the balcony. A few of the guys inside were already passed out, the rest playing some video game on the big screen TV in the room. I could tell by Beau's stance that he was pretty tipsy, though not too far gone.

"What's up, big man?"

"Mind if we talk?"

I gestured to the spot next to me against the balcony rail. "Don't mind at all. What's going on?"

"Nothing. Just thinking about the wedding."

"Good things, I hope?"

He nodded, leaning against the railing next to me, a half-drunk beer in his hands.

"Good things. But still, it's so weird knowing that I've only got a few more days of being a single guy left, right? I'm excited about the wedding, but... it's still so surreal."

"I know, bud. I've been there. You spend your adult life single, then you're in love, then you're planning a wedding, and then... life happens. Hell, it's all life, even the parts where it just feels like you're planning and waiting for the 'real' stuff to begin."

"I love her, Dad. Man, I really love her."

I chuckled. "Someone's drunk."

He grinned sheepishly. "Yeah. Maybe I am. But damn, even throughout the wedding planning, I still love her like crazy. More and more each day, actually."

"Good. That's how it should feel, like you're caught up in something amazing and terrifying all at once, because that's what it is."

Silence fell, the two of us watching the city and sipping our drinks.

"And... I know it doesn't do me any good to think this way, but planning the wedding just makes me miss Mom even more." His voice choked up a bit. I was normally the kind of man who tried to keep my emotions in check in front of others, but the subject of Charlotte was enough to make even my throat tight.

"Kid, I know exactly what you mean. Your mom... she loved you like mad, even though she didn't get to spend much time with you. But the way she looked at you, the way she held you with love in her eyes..." I had to take a moment, sipping my whiskey to give myself a chance to regain my composure. "It would've been the best day of her life to see you get married to a woman you loved, start a family of your own."

"Yeah. God, I wish I could've known her."

"I do too. But son, don't you ever forget that she's here with us, looking down, happy as hell with the way our lives are going."

"I bet she'd even be happy that you've found someone," he said. "If even half of what you told me about her is true, then I bet anything she'd want you to love someone again."

Just thinking about it hurt. I hadn't quite wrapped my head around the fact that I was on the verge of starting another life with another woman. But Beau was right—all Charlotte wanted was for the ones she loved to be happy. And she'd always have a place in my heart.

"I think you're right. But this isn't about me, kid, it's about you. You're the groom, you're the one getting hitched. You feeling good? Excited?"

He smiled. "Yeah. Drunk, but excited."

I nodded toward the room. "Then do tomorrow-you a

favor and get some sleep, don't make that hangover any worse than it needs to be."

"I will. Thanks for talking, Dad. I love you."

"I love you, son." I opened my arms and the two of us gave one another a back-clapping hug. "Get some sleep."

I clapped down on Beau's shoulder one last time, my boy smiling at me before turning and heading inside. I turned my attention back to the city, feeling a little lighter.

CHAPTER 28

BETH

It was the day of the wedding, and it was already shaping up to be a total disaster.

"Hi. Hi?" I paced back and forth in the lobby of the lodge, seemingly everyone there watching me. "Is this Sure-Thing Plowing?"

"It *sure* is." The voice on the other end of the line let out a laugh, as if they never got enough of making that joke.

"OK, great. My name's Beth Wheeler, and I've got a wedding up at the Crested Butte Lodge. I was wondering if it would be possible for you guys to, well, plow the way up?"

I stepped over to one of the big, arched windows overlooking the front of the lodge property. The sky was blanketed in deceptively white and friendly-looking clouds. The snow had been coming at a slow pace and was supposed to stop the previous night after a few inches but it didn't. Instead, it kept coming and kept coming, and when I'd woken up that morning, refreshed and ready to tackle the weekend ahead, I'd thrown open the curtains to our room at the lodge only to be greeted with snow.

Tons of snow.

The entire front of the property was blanketed, not a single car visible under the thick white. While I couldn't make out the road leading to the lodge from my room's window, there'd been no doubt in my mind that it was a mess.

"Well, about that," spoke the receptionist. "We're slammed from the snowfall last night. All of our trucks are already out servicing places around town. Doesn't the lodge have its own snow plow setup?"

"They do, but they're more concerned with making sure the property is cleared for the guests already here than plowing the road leading to the lodge. And the city doesn't exactly consider it a priority to make sure people can get here."

"That's how it goes sometimes. Good luck!"

The call ended before I had a chance to say another word. I let out a frustrated sigh as I shoved my phone back into my pocket. The calm of the lobby was a total contrast to the frenzy that Megan was in the middle of when I came back to the ballroom.

"This is so unfair!"

Even with Megan screeching in the background, I had to take a moment to appreciate how damned incredible the ballroom looked. The decorators had pulled off the tunnel idea perfectly, guests entering through a tunnel of purple, white, and pink Colorado flowers that opened up to the majesty of the room. Each table was set, the gorgeous little centerpieces arranged just how Megan had wanted them.

Off to the right was the dance floor and DJ booth, the bar beyond that. To the left were the doors that led to the outdoor courtyard where the altar was set up, Megan and Celina insisting on an outdoor ceremony despite the weather. That, too, was stunning, that is, when it wasn't blanketed in snow. A long buffet table was set up, the space prepared for a grand lunch that would never happen, the staff standing by to serve guests who would, in all likelihood, never come.

The day was looking to be a total catastrophe. Some of the guests, mostly immediate family, had chosen to stay in the lodge, and thus were present and accounted for. The vast majority had been planning to drive up that morning. The unanticipated snowfall meant that, barring a freaking miracle, they wouldn't be able to get there.

"There has to be something we can do!" Megan stomped around the room, going from her mom to her dad to Beau, as if one of them might have the answer for how the wedding could be saved. When she spotted me entering, her eyes flashed. "Beth! What happened? What did the plow people say?"

"No go," I replied. "Every plow in the city's booked up."

Megan regarded me with wide eyes for a moment, finally letting out a cry of frustration that filled the entire space, everyone there wincing.

"No, no way! I *refuse* to believe that my wedding, my actual, freaking wedding, is going to be ruined because of some stupid *snow!*"

"Hon," Beau said, raising his palms as he moved toward her as if he were approaching a rabid raccoon. "Getting upset isn't going to help anything. Right now, we kind of have to, you know... roll with the punches."

Megan froze in place, her eyes going even wider. "Did you just say, '*roll with the punches?*' This is supposed to be the biggest, most important day of my life, and you want me to *roll with the punches?*"

"That's what he said." Jack's deep voice carried through

the ballroom, all of us turning to watch as he ducked out of the flower-covered tunnel.

Jack looked *amazing*. He was dressed in a classic tux, his hair slicked back, and his oh-so-sexy salt-and-pepper beard trimmed. It was like he'd gone from mountain man to James Bond over the course of the morning and it did all kinds of things to me.

"Whatever," Megan pouted. "The point is there's no getting over this. It's ruined!"

Beau, not one to be deterred, went over to her, saying something quietly as he tried to lead Megan away from the eyes and ears of the two dozen or so people in the room. Jack stepped to my side, chuckling a bit as he approached.

"Sorry," he said. "I shouldn't be laughing. This is bad for you, too."

"You know, it is what it is. I'm not happy it looks like the wedding isn't going to go off without a hitch, but that's what this business is all about, right? Planning not just for one thing, but for *everything* that could happen."

"Now that's a good attitude. What're you thinking for our distraught bride?"

I sighed, Jack asking the question that had been on my mind for the last two hours.

"Well, first step is to let her calm down. She's upset, and rightly so. This *is* her big day, after all." As I spoke, Megan's parents approached, expressions of interest on their faces. No doubt they wanted to know what I had in mind for salvaging the day.

"Next, we scale back." I flicked my eyes to Celina, Megan's mom. "What's the arrival count?"

"Twenty, besides us—extended family who flew in and decided to stay at the lodge."

"So, that's about two dozen altogether. That's not nearly

the hundred we'd planned for, but that's more than enough for a more intimate wedding. That's the word we're going for here... intimate."

My mind was racing with ideas. "First, we do a nice, low-key lunch." I glanced over to Maritza. "The restaurant has a private party room, right?"

"That's right. And it's available now, I believe."

"Perfect. Instead of doing a big luncheon in here, let's reserve the private room and have it set up for a smaller crowd. We'll do a nice little lunch, give all the guests here a chance to spend some time together in a more laid-back setting. After that we'll take a break, let the guests relax and enjoy the lodge for a bit before the ceremony at three. Once that's done, it's cocktails, and then a more subdued dinner, maybe push the tables together so everyone can see everyone else's beautiful faces up close and personal and not across the room."

"That sounds really nice," Celina said, relieved by my little off-the-dome spiel.

"Right," Martin said, nodding along in agreement. "Big weddings are always so chaotic, you never get a chance to spend time with anyone. This, ah, more intimate setup sounds a little more my speed."

After he finished speaking, Maritza waved from across the room to get my attention. I smiled and nodded, and she hurried over with her phone in her hand.

"OK, just got word that the plows are going to be clearing the road up to the lodge this afternoon. If all goes well, they'll have it cleared and ready to drive on by three or four."

Relief washed over me at the news. It wasn't the best situation, but it meant that we might be able to salvage the evening.

"That's *perfect*," I said. "We can send out the news to the guests, retool the menu so it's a buffet style that'll be more amenable to people coming in whenever they can get here. And by the time the evening arrives, we can get the dance party started!"

I glanced up, realizing I'd gotten so wrapped up in my plans that I hadn't even noticed that Megan had been watching and listening. Her eyes still glistened with tears and were red all the way around, but she'd stopped crying, stopped throwing a fit.

"That could work," she said.

In fact, everyone who was in the room had gathered around in a half-circle, hanging on my every word as I dished out orders. I felt amazing, like a general commanding my army.

"What're you all standing around for?" I asked. "We have a wedding to get ready for!"

∼

We had a nice lunch in the lodge restaurant, the twenty-two guests who'd had rooms at the lodge all attending. Just as I'd hoped, it was an intimate affair, the privacy of the party room allowing everyone to relax and cut loose, the family sharing stories and catching up.

After lunch, we broke for the afternoon while the bride and groom got ready for the big ceremony ahead. The rest of the guests were free to chill, and I was close by to supervise everything, making sure we were ready for the ceremony and the dinner after.

At around one-thirty, we received the best news we could've hoped for—the plows had arrived early. The lodge premises had been cleared by that point too, and between the lodge plows going down and the city ones coming up, it didn't take long at all until the winding road up to Crested Butte was open once more. The family fired off texts, letting the rest of the guests know that the evening was still set to go.

The ceremony was beautiful, the outdoor space warmed by well-placed space heaters, the valley spread out before us. Nearly all of the guests had arrived in time, and the ones that hadn't were on their way. By the time Beau and Megan were done reading their adorably corny self-written vows, there wasn't a dry eye in the house.

The cocktail hour was the last push of preparation. I spent the time zipping through the ballroom, making sure every last detail was in order before the dinner and party after. Before too long, guests streamed in, meals were served, and toasts were made. A little after that, the DJ started playing his set, the guests getting up one by one to shake their butts on the dance floor. Even Jack, looking so freaking sexy in his tux that it hurt to look at him, busted out some surprisingly good moves.

It was then, and only then, that I allowed myself a small moment of relaxation. Jack seemed to sense it, approaching me with a glass of whiskey in one hand, a clear drink with a lime in the other.

"Can I tempt a hard-working woman with a club soda and lime?" he asked.

"God, that sounds like heaven." I took the drink, holding the cool glass to my head for a moment.

Jack leaned against the wall next to me, the two of us looking out over the party. The sun was well into setting in the west, the sky full of wild oranges and purples. The snow from the morning glittered, making the scene all the more beautiful.

"I think this deserves a toast," he said, holding out his glass of whiskey.

"Night's not over yet, but I'll take it."

We tapped glasses and drank.

"Listen," he said. "I had no doubt that you'd be able to pull this thing off. You're brilliant and creative and you've got a good mind for details that people like me don't even think of. But watching you actually do it, watching you get a handle on a potential disaster, calm down a worried bride, and right the ship... that was impressive as hell."

I smiled. "Thanks, Jack. It was looking dire there for a second, but I think I pulled it off. And you all helped too, don't sell yourself short.

"You kidding? I just followed orders. You were the mastermind behind this operation. You deserve all the credit and you're going to get it. I've been hearing people talk about how amazing this wedding's been, wondering who the planner was behind it. Got a feeling this is the start of a long, successful career for you. Nice work."

I was trying to play it cool, but hearing all the good news coming from Jack was making me feel an intense excitement about my future.

"I'm happy that you're here with me," I said.

He leaned over and planted a kiss on my lips. "You know I feel the same way. Love you, gorgeous."

"Love you too, handsome."

We both looked up to see Beau and Megan, along with her parents and a few other members of the family, waving for us to come over.

"Think that means it's our turn on the dance floor," he said.

"Save a place for me. I think I need a few minutes of fresh air."

"Sure thing." With that, he put his hand on my hip and gave it a squeeze before heading off to the dance floor.

I weaved my way through the crowd and out onto the outdoor balcony behind the ballroom. A dozen or so people were out there, sipping drinks and chatting quietly to one another, taking a break from the raucous music and dancing inside.

I craned my neck and spotted the turn of the balcony where it went to the other side of the lodge. Club soda in hand, I headed around.

Just as I'd hoped, the spot was quiet, totally empty. I flicked on a nearby space heater and leaned against the railing. Down to my right, I could see where the balcony led to the front parking lot, the faint sounds of cars driving and tires crunching over snow and salt.

I sipped my drink and looked out over the valley, letting Jack's words play in my mind. I was never one to get ahead of myself, but I couldn't help but get a little enlivened at what he'd told me. Part of me had been certain that the wedding was going to be a disaster, one way or another. But I'd found my nerve, called the shots, and turned a potential disaster into something amazing, if I did say so myself.

Not to mention everything else that I had to be excited about. Jack, the twins... I couldn't wait to get started. A big smile on my face, I took one more sip of my drink and prepared to head back inside.

"Now, now, now," spoke a familiar voice. "If it isn't just the lady I've been looking for."

I froze, knowing who the voice belonged to. A chill of horror running through me, I turned slowly to see none other than Michael Schafer with two hulking goons at his sides approach, a sinister grin on his face that made it clear this perfect evening was about to take a horrible turn.

CHAPTER 29

BETH

His smile was predatory as he approached. My eyes flicked to the man at Schafer's right, a total colossus of a human, his height a good foot over Michael, his shoulders as broad as the front of a damn car.

Michael raised his palms as he approached.

"Now, I know what you're thinking, there's nothing worse than party crashers, right? But listen, I'm only here to talk."

I wanted to run; I wanted to scream; I wanted to do *something*. Maybe it was the fact that I wasn't just worried about my own life, but I couldn't move so much as a muscle. I was terrified, more scared than I'd ever been.

"There we go," Michael said, sensing my frozen fear. "Let's keep things nice and calm. We're not here to wreck the wedding, we're just here to talk and sort out some business matters with you, that's it. Just a little conversation is all. Got it?"

As he spoke, however, the enormous goon moved around me, taking position at the part of the balcony from where I'd come, blocking any possible escape. I felt so helpless, totally locked in fear as that part of the balcony wasn't visible from the ballroom windows. Nobody inside had any idea of what was going on.

Michael approached, leaning against the railing and taking a small flask out of his inner coat pocket, removing the top and bringing it to his lips as he looked out over the valley.

"Gorgeous, isn't it? Views like this never fail to remind me why Colorado is so damn special. The bosses back in New York thought I was crazy for wanting to move here and set up shop. But one look at a view like this and I know I made the right call." He shook his head, clucking his tongue in appreciation before taking one more sip, then putting his flask away.

"What do you want?" The paralyzing fear faded by the moment, and I was finding my spine. Still, the fact that my babies were in danger kept me in a state of high-adrenaline alertness that I'd never known before.

"I want to talk," he said. "That's it."

"Then talk."

I considered screaming for help. But the presence of the men sent a clear message—do anything that Michael doesn't explicitly tell you to, and there will be consequences. There was no doubt in my mind that Michael was a killer, that he'd have no problems hurting me, pregnant or not, if it might help him get what he wanted.

He flashed me another scheming smile, his eyes going down to my belly.

"How are the twins? Getting bigger by the day, no doubt. How excited you must be to know motherhood is just around the corner. That is, if you play ball."

Threatening me was one thing, threatening my children was another. The fear vanished, replaced by pure anger.

"If you say one more word about my children, I'll rip your fucking head off. Got it?"

The group of men all made the same *ooohhh* noises in response to my threat. I was angry, filled with more fury than I'd ever felt before. I didn't give a shit that there were three of them, didn't give a shit that they were all bigger than me. If they came near me, I'd go down clawing their eyes out.

"I can see you're a little upset," Michael chided. "So, I'll get right to the point. Got word from a little bird that Jacky's working behind my back, talking to the Feds about the job I need him to do. That's... not good. I trusted the guy, and hearing that he's planning to betray me? It broke my heart." He grinned. "Believe it or not, I've got one of those."

"What do *I* have to do with this?"

"You kidding? If I want to get to him, going through you is the best way to do it. So, that's why I'm here." He stepped closer to me, his face going from pretend friendly to menacing. "You're going to come with me, beautiful. And you're going to stay with me until Jack tells the FBI to screw off and does what I say. Understand?"

Fear filled me once more at the realization that he'd come there to kidnap me.

"You do this the easy way, and no one gets hurt. You come with me, I take a few pictures to send to Jack to let him know what's at stake, and he does the job. Jack's a smart guy—he'll do the right thing. Then, when I'm happy with the work, I'll send you back and you two can have your little happy ending. Sound good?"

I stood firm. "Not a chance. I'm not going anywhere with you."

Michael laughed. "Funny you say that like you've got a

choice." He nodded to the man behind me. "You so much take a step without my say so, and I'll—"

He didn't get a chance to finish his sentence. I pulled my hand back and brought it hard against his face, a *crack* sounding out as palm hit cheek. Michael's head whipped to the side from my strike, and I stood with a shaking hand in the air as he turned back to face me.

Pure anger formed on his face. Then, before I had a chance to say or do anything, he raised his hand with surprising speed, hitting me with a smack of his own. Pain shot through me, hot and stinging and enough to make me drop to my knees.

"Stupid move," he growled as he loomed over me. "Stupid, *stupid* fucking move." He glanced over to the towering man. "Grab her now; she's coming with us."

The man didn't get a chance. A battle cry sounded out, and we all turned just in time to watch as Jack rushed from around the corner, righteous anger like war paint on his face.

CHAPTER 30

JACK

Pure instinct took over as I flew toward the goon. I'd come around the corner just in time to see Michael hit Beth, and all I could think about was ripping each one of those pricks to shreds.

The man nearest to me was hulking, easily around six and a half feet tall, but I didn't give a damn. I put my shoulder forward and slammed into him as hard as I could, knocking the wind from his belly and sending him staggering backward into the railing. He hit it hard enough to put him in a daze.

"Jack!" Beth shrieked my name, sticking out her hand. Michael was too quick for her, grabbing Beth by the shoulder and pulling her back behind the other man. The second thug wasn't quite as big as the first, but the ugly scars on his face made it clear he was no stranger to violence.

I rushed toward him, ducking a fist coming in from the side and delivering a driving punch right to the fucker's breadbasket. He let out a *whoomph* of air and staggered backward, doing his best to quickly compose himself for another strike.

I closed the distance between us but was greeted with a sharp jab to the face that he was able to pull off with surprising speed. I stumbled a step back, my vision blurry but clear enough to see his next intended attack, a punch aimed at my neck. I caught that one, gripping his fist as hard as I could and squeezing it tightly. He let out a cry of pain, and I would've pulverized every last bone in his hand had he not managed to raise his foot and deliver a kick to my knee.

"Jack! Look out!"

Beth called to me, and I glanced over my shoulder, watching with horror as the enormous man struggled to his feet, shaking his head as he came back to reality. I needed to take him down, and fast—there was no way I'd be able to handle both of the men on my own.

I stepped forward, connecting my fists to the shorter man's stomach with a hard barrage of punches, one-two-three. He let out a groan of pain as he lumbered back, his eyes wide from the shock of the attack. I was about to move in and give him one more solid punch to the face, one that would surely have knocked him on his ass, but another scream from Beth pulled my attention once more over my shoulder.

I glanced back just in time to watch as the enormous man lumbered toward me, his mouth in a hard line, his shaved head catching the glint of lights above us. I was ready to fight to the last, but then a voice rang out in the air.

"Hey, shithead!"

The entire group turned to look in the direction of the voice. I knew right away who it was, I'd recognize that voice anywhere.

Beau stepped around the corner, a menacing look on his face. There was no doubt in my mind that he was ready to fight, but I knew my son. He was tough, built solid and packed serious strength. But he wasn't a fighter, he'd never had to be. If Beau was going to tangle with the wall of muscle between us, there was a damn good chance he'd walk away with some significant damage.

That is, if he'd be able to walk away at all.

"Beau!" I shouted. "Get back, now!"

"No fucking way!" he shot back. Without another word, he stormed toward the giant man, leaping into the air and grabbing onto him, both going down in a heap.

"Ah, shit!" It was too late to do anything about it then. Beau and the giant man were locked in a grappling match, one in which neither of them had the upper hand. Best I could hope for was that Beau could hold his own until I took out the other guy.

I turned my attention to the goon I'd been tangling with, who'd thankfully been just as wrapped up in the sudden fight between the giant and my boy as I had. But when I locked eyes with him, the insidious grin on his face let me know that the fight was back on. He reached into his coat, pulling out a small switchblade.

"Fucking hell." I muttered the words under my breath. I'd seen enough violence in my day to know that a knife, however small, could make the difference between a rough fight and a deadly one.

He ran toward me, raising the knife over his head as if he were a knight ready to cut through a dragon. Lucky for me, I knew taking big swipes with a small blade like that was about the dumbest thing you could do.

His over-the-top form gave me all the time I needed to prepare a defense. He swung down hard, just as I'd anticipated. I stepped aside, letting his momentum carry him all the way down. I allowed myself a small grin, knowing he was right where I wanted him. Once the blade was pointed toward the ground, I moved in, putting one hand on his shoulder and the other on his head, giving him a shove and slamming the side of his head hard into the railing. A *crack* sounded out as his thick skull cracked the wood, the man tumbling down into a heap.

I caught my breath, making sure the goon was out. But another shout from Beau brought my attention back to the tussle taking place behind me. I couldn't believe what I saw when I turned. The fight was no longer one-on-one, it was *three*-on-one.

A goddamn crowd had poured around the corner, some of the groomsmen joining the fray as the rest watched from a safe distance. Beau and his buds slammed the big ape with one fist after another, the barrage slowly but surely bringing the man down.

"Get his ass!" I shouted. I wanted to get in for a hit, but with the frenzy that was going on, I would've done more harm than good.

Blow by blow, the groomsmen brought the man down. Even Martin arrived on the scene to get in a smack or two. More of a crowd formed, Megan standing in her wedding dress among them, her hands covering her mouth in total shock.

Another scream pulled my attention back to Beth and Michael. There was panic on his face as he held her close, his expression revealing that his plan wasn't at all going the way he'd hoped. The anger returned, and he grabbed onto Beth hard as she tried to struggle away. I started toward them, ready to lay his ass out and end it once and for all.

The silver flash of a pistol pulled out of his coat stopped me in my tracks. He grinned, pointing the gun at Beth.

"Now, I don't need to tell you how bad of an idea it

would be to try anything, Jacky," he said. "Do what you want with those assholes, but I'm taking her with me, got it? Take so much as a single *step* and I'll put one in her, then one in you. Because there's not a chance I'm going to let you take me down, understand?"

"Don't hurt her, Michael," I said. "It's over. You don't need to make this worse for yourself."

"The only way this is going to get worse is if you don't do what I say, got it? Now, step away right fucking now, or I'll—"

He didn't get a chance to finish. Beth pulled her free arm forward and slammed it back, her elbow jabbing right into his gut. Michael's eyes went wide, the gun falling from his hand and onto the ground, the pair stumbling toward the railing.

All I could do was yell "no!" as they fell over the side.

CHAPTER 31

BETH

Everything swirled around me as I toppled over the balcony railing, the whole scene becoming somehow even more surreal. Through the chaos, however, I spotted Jack rushing toward me, reaching out his arm and grabbing me by the wrist.

I came to an immediate stop, shrieks of horror sounding from the rest of the guests as they saw what was happening. When I looked around, I realized that I was dangling over the valley down below, the drop easily a few thousand feet. Endless white was beneath me, and there was no freaking doubt that if I were to fall, that'd be it for me, and the twins.

"Hang on, Beth!" Jack had my wrist, but at an awkward angle that barely allowed him to keep his grip. To my right, Michael was hanging on for dear life himself, his hands gripping the bottom ledge of the balcony right by the base of the wood slats.

"Help me!" he cried out. "I'm slipping!"

Not a soul paid attention to him. Jack stared down at me with worried eyes, his arm straining from my weight.

"You gotta give me your other arm," he said. "I don't

know if this barrier can support me leaning against it like this."

Sure enough, a crack formed in the wood. Jack's size wasn't doing him any favors in the situation we were in. No doubt the railing hadn't been designed to support a man his size plus a woman pregnant with twins.

Fatigue ran through me, the fight with Michael having sapped my energy.

"Come on!" he shouted. "Grab onto me!"

I closed my eyes, doing the best I could to ignore the fear running through me, to not think about the fact that one wrong move would mean me landing two-thousand feet below. I summoned what little strength I had left, reaching my arm up and toward Jack.

"There you go! There!"

Once my hand was up a little bit more, he reached around with his other and grabbed hold. Just then the crack in the wood grew and deepened.

"Jack! It's not going to hold!"

"Yes, it will!"

Both of my hands in his grasp, he pulled as hard as he could, the crack spreading. Just as it looked as if the railing might break and send both of us tumbling down the side of the valley, Beau rushed over and grabbed ahold of his dad by the shoulders, pulling as hard as he could.

"Come on, old man!" he yelled. "Come on!"

Beau was just the extra bit of strength we needed. He pulled Jack, Jack pulled me, and together we went back up and over the rail. A collective sigh of relief sounded out when the crowd watching realized that I was OK. I sat on the ground, catching my breath as the pure insanity of what had just happened washed over me.

"Help!" Michael's voice cutting through the air reminded all of us that it wasn't over yet.

I stood, looking over the balcony and seeing that Michael was still hanging off. Red and blue flashing lights in the parking lot let me know that the cops had arrived, one of the guests likely having put the call in when it became known what was happening.

Jack and Beau stepped next to me, looking down.

"You know," Jack said. "I've got a good mind to let your ass fall, you miserable old prick. You come to my son's wedding and threaten my family. There's a special place in hell for men like you."

"But you're not going to do that, right?" asked Michael, pure, fearful panic in his voice. "You're a good man!"

"I try to be," he said. "And it's a damn good thing I do. The world needs decent people to stand up to thugs like you."

If Jack wanted Michael to drop, all he'd have to do was simply nothing at all. Instead, he reached down and grabbed Michael's hand, Beau coming over to get the other. Together, they pulled him up just in time to heave him over the banister and into the arms of the waiting police. The cops took Michael away, Jack mentioning Michael's gun to one of the officers who picked it up from the ground and tucked it safely away.

Jack came over and wrapped his arms around me.

"It's alright, baby. We're going to be OK."

∽

"Now, tell me how many fingers I'm holding up."

It was an hour later, and I was up in the lodge's clinic.

"Three. Come on now, I didn't get brain damage."

The nurse, a heavyset woman with a friendly tone and professional attitude, raised her eyebrows at me.

"Sorry," I said. "Just shaken up. And the babies…"

I placed my hand on my belly. It wasn't as if I'd landed on my middle or taken a punch there, but all the same I was so worried about what the stress might have done to my babies that I couldn't think straight.

"Easy," Jack consoled, placing his hand on my shoulder. "They're just doing their jobs."

"I know you're worried," the nurse said. "But we're having someone get the heartbeat doppler out of storage. Not something we use all that often at a ski lodge."

Right as she said the words, one of the clinic staff came into the room, a plastic bin in her hands.

"Got it," she said. "Put some fresh batteries in it, too."

"Thanks, Sammy." The nurse wasted no time getting the thing set up, testing it to make sure it worked and then bringing it over to me. "Alright, so we're listening for two heartbeats, right?"

I nodded. I was so scared, so worried that something might've happened to my twins, that I couldn't even speak. Jack said nothing, keeping his hand on my shoulder as the nurse set up the doppler, placing the receiving end on my belly after having me lay down and pull up my shirt.

At first, there was silence. A fear like nothing I'd ever known before shot through me at the idea of the trauma that I'd just gone through having hurt the babies, maybe even…

I didn't even want to think about it.

"Sorry," the nurse said. "Been a long time since I've used one of these."

The nurse moved the wand around until the most beautiful sound in the world filled the room.

Whomp-whomp-whomp.

The familiar super-fast beating of two hearts. I cried. I couldn't help it. The babies were safe, Jack was safe, and so was I.

"There we are, darlin'," he said, giving my hand another squeeze. "Looks like we got through all of this just fine."

We finished up in the clinic, the nurse applying a few band-aids here and there where my skin had been scuffed by the fall over the rail. When we were done, Jack helped me up and out of the clinic. My mom and dad were waiting for us in the hallway, both of them hugging me like crazy and covering me in kisses. I was thankful to Jack for calling them.

"Careful! Babies and bruises to worry about."

"Sorry, sorry," Dad said. "Just that... God, you were hanging from the *balcony*?"

"How on earth did you even get mixed up in something like that?" Mom asked.

Jack rubbed the back of his neck. "Uh, I can fill you both in but right now, I think it's a good idea to let her get some rest."

They agreed, and Jack took me up to the room we'd rented, the view gorgeous and the silence enough to calm me down a bit. He eased me onto the bed, my muscles crying out in relief at the softness of the mattress.

Once I was down, Jack put his hands on his hips and looked me over.

"What a goddamn day," he said. "But here we are, together."

His words put a smile on my face. "Yeah. We're together."

"Listen, I ought to go talk to your parents. And I need to make a call to the FBI. But I don't want to leave you alone."

"I'll be fine."

A knock sounded at the door.

Jack flashed me a curious look before heading over and glancing through the peephole. He let out a chuckle and smiled at the sight of whoever it was on the other side.

"It's Megan," he said. "Want me to tell her to come back later?"

I smiled, shaking my head. "Nah, send the blushing bride in."

He opened the door, Megan on the other side still in her wedding dress, a somewhat sheepish expression on her face.

"Now," Jack started. "It's been a while since my own wedding night, but I'm pretty sure you're supposed to be spending it with someone other than your planner."

Megan laughed. "Beau's still with his buds going over all the highlights of the fight. He's good for now. Besides, I wanted to talk to Beth if that's alright."

"I was just about to head down to debrief her parents. And I'd feel a hell of a lot better leaving her in your hands than all by her lonesome."

"Well, I'd be more than happy to keep her company. Besides, I have some things I want to say to her."

Jack glanced in my direction with his eyebrows raised, as if giving me one more chance to tell him that I'd actually rather be alone.

"I'll be alright. Go."

Jack nodded then smiled, stepping over and kissing me on the forehead.

"You need me, I'm a text away."

With that, he gave my hand a squeeze, then headed out.

Megan pursed her lips once the door was shut, as if not sure where to begin. Thing was, *I* had something I wanted to say, too.

"Listen," I said. "I'm so, so, *so* sorry that your wedding

got wrapped up in all of this insanity. Last thing you ought to be dealing with is attempted murder while you're trying to have a good time."

"Are you kidding? My wedding's going to be the talk of the freaking town now! And it wasn't ruined at all! Everyone's down there hitting up the open bar and working off the adrenaline on the dance floor while swapping stories of what they were doing when it happened. And shoot, Beau and the guys are going to be bragging about this for the next ten years. Heck, I bet he'll be telling our *kids* about it... when we have kids, that is."

She stepped over to the desk chair, turned it toward me, and sat down.

"No, you didn't ruin my wedding. In fact, you're the one who saved it. I don't know what would've happened if you hadn't been here to snap me out of it and plan something after we got snowed in. You're really good at this."

"Thanks, Megan."

"That's what I wanted to come here to say. Ever since high school, I've been this mean little brat to you for no reason. And these last couple months with you busting your butt to make my wedding the most amazing it could be... you'd think I would've calmed it down. But no. Instead, I treated you like some kind of punching bag. It was totally unfair, and totally out of line. And that's to say nothing of me blurting out your secret."

She sighed, looking away.

"So, I wanted to apologize. I wanted to tell you I'm sorry for treating you the way that I did. And I wanted to say *thank you so much* for making this day so special."

"Even if it involved a near-death experience?"

She laughed. "Even then."

"Thanks," I said. "I appreciate it."

"Any chance for a toast?" she stepped over to the mini bar, taking out a small bottle of sparkling cider.

"I'd love nothing more."

I rose from the bed. Megan and I stepped over to the window and poured ourselves glasses of cider, the beauty of the valley before us.

"To new beginnings," she said.

"I'll drink to that."

CHAPTER 32

JACK

By the time I was done explaining the situation to Mr. and Mrs. Wheeler, I was ready for a drink. They'd calmed down some, especially after they'd gotten a chance to speak to Beth and confirm that she hadn't been totally traumatized. All the same, it wasn't easy explaining to the future grandparents of your kids that you were, once upon a time, a mobster, kind of.

"Well, that's one way to end a case."

I glanced over to the seat next to me to watch as Agent Miller sat down. I got the bartender's attention, and he quickly came over.

"Drinks on me. That is, if Uncle Sam doesn't mind."

"Why not? I'm off the clock until DPD's done with him. A vodka martini, please, extra lemon."

Moments later, we had our drinks, tapping them together in celebration of the bust.

"So, what's the story with Michael?"

"He's being processed right now. Once that's taken care of, we start the back and forth of getting his ass into federal custody. That's never fun, but once he's in our hands, we can get the indictment going."

"Good to hear. But what I want to know is whether or not we ever have to worry about his miserable ass bothering us again."

"We've got some dirt on him, and he's got a long criminal record. Attempted kidnapping is enough to put him away for a while. And that's not all. Michael was the head of the Tuvatti crime family here in Denver. With him behind bars, we're going to have a hell of a lot less crime to worry about down the line. My informants back in New York are already reporting that the rest of the syndicate is strongly considering writing off Denver. Too hot here now for them."

"Well, that's a nice little bonus."

"And just in case you were wondering, there's no file on you. Well, not anymore, at least. Statute of limitations is up on pretty much anything you could get tagged for, and I'll be around to make sure no one does any sniffing around until the rest of them are expired."

"Thanks. I mean it."

She took a sip of her drink. "Least I could do." Her phone on the bar buzzed, and she leaned forward to check the screen. "Shoot, my supervisor. Gotta take this."

Agent Miller prepared to get up, but I stopped her. "You take the bar. I ought to make my rounds back at the reception."

"Got it. And congrats, by the way. Not just about your son getting hitched either. I heard about the twins. Mama doing OK?"

I flashed her a smile. "Thanks. And she's doing just fine, getting a little rest upstairs. See you around, Agent Miller."

She responded with a playful salute before answering

her phone and tending to her call. Drink in hand, I made my way back to the ballroom, where the reception was still underway. Megan was there, shaking her butt in the middle of the dance floor, dozens of friends and family there with her. I wondered what her conversation with Beth had been about.

I looked around, but there was no sign of Beau. I scanned the room, spotting him out on the balcony. A few moments later, I was there with him.

"Hey, kid."

He glanced over his shoulder, drink in hand. "Hey, Pops."

I stepped to his side and clapped my hand down onto his back. He winced as I did. "You OK?"

"Fine. Mostly. When the boys and I brought down that ape-in-a-suit he kinda landed on my chest. They think it might be a bruised rib, nothing to worry about."

I chuckled. "See, that's why you leave that sort of thing to the pros."

He grinned, looking me up and down. "Would've thought you'd have been in traction from that little scuffle. Old codger like you is likely to break a hip."

That got a loud laugh out of me. "Seriously though, Beau. I appreciate what you did. That was damn brave of you."

"Not all that brave to pounce on a huge guy with a bunch of my friends. But we got the job done."

I laughed. "Damn, sometimes you remind me so much of me that it's scary."

He cocked his head to the side. "What're you talking about?"

"Downplaying what you did, playing up your friends. Good quality to have if I do say so myself. And I get it—you don't like being in the center spotlight, no desire for that kind of attention."

He said nothing as I spoke, sipping his beer and nodding along to my words.

"All the same, you ought to know when you've done the right thing, and when you've done something brave."

He gave me a subdued smile. "Thanks, Dad." Beau turned where he stood, watching the crowd through the windows. Megan was still there, dancing and having the time of her life. "Speaking of brave... got to admit I'm a little worried about this marriage thing."

"Hate to point out that it might be a little too late for that, son."

Beau chuckled. "I love Megan, don't get me wrong. I'm just worried about being a good husband, whether or not I've got what it takes. And that's to say nothing about being a *dad*. How the hell do I know I'm going to be good at it?"

"I know you, son. And I know you're gonna kick ass at both. But if you ask me, you *are* making a big mistake right now."

"What's that?"

I nodded to the window. "Letting that beautiful bride of yours dance all by herself. Get in there, kid, you've got a lot to celebrate today."

"Thanks, Dad."

Beau and I hugged one more time before he headed inside. I watched as he joined Megan on the dance floor, her face lighting up as he approached. They wasted no time joining together, giving one another a kiss before starting their dance.

Damn, was I proud.

"Room for one more out here?"

I glanced over to see Beth approaching. "Hey now, you're supposed to be resting in the room," I gently chided.

She nodded toward the party inside. "I'm fine, the twins are fine, and I've got a job to do."

I chuckled. "Now, that's the kind of work ethic I like in a woman. You sure you're feeling up to it?"

She nodded. "I'm sure."

I couldn't help but admire the hell out of her. "I know you're on the clock, but you got time for a dance?"

Inside the music began to slow down, changing to something more appropriate to hold someone close to.

She smiled warmly. "I think I can squeeze it in. Especially for a guest as handsome as you."

I offered her my hand, and she took it. "Let's get in there, then. I want to show you off."

EPILOGUE I

BETH

Four and a half months later...

I was on the balcony of our new apartment when I felt the first twinge.

It was a picture-perfect day, and I'd spent it guiding the movers, telling them where to place the brand-new furnishings that I'd spent the last month going over. After Jack and I moved in together, we'd decided that just a place in the woods, nice as it was, wouldn't do. I was a city girl, after all, with a job that required me to be in town a good chunk of the time.

Rather than try to sell the cabin, especially when it would be such a nice place to have for weekend getaways, we'd decided that getting a place in the city was the thing to do. We picked out the gorgeous penthouse in a new building downtown that had an amazing view of the city to the north.

I staggered into the apartment, my hand on my belly.

One of the movers looked up at me, a huge box in his hands.

"Uh, miss? You OK?"

"I'm... good." The words came out in such an awkward way that there had to have been no doubt that things weren't actually good at all. "Can you..."

As much as I didn't want to freak out, I decided that it would be majorly stupid to try to pretend that nothing was wrong. I closed my eyes, took a breath, and spoke.

"OK, I don't want to put any pressure on you, or make you do something that's not part of your job, but..."

His eyes flashed. "You're having that baby, aren't you?"

I nodded slowly. "Yep. Well, twins actually."

"Oh, shit! OK, what can I do?"

"Can... can you get my phone while I sit down? It's in the kitchen."

"Say no more."

I stepped into the big living room space, afternoon light pouring in as I sat down on the huge, U-shaped sectional couch. I gave myself a few moments to catch my breath, the strange, aching pain nearly stealing it away.

It didn't take long before the mover came over with my phone and a bottle of water, setting them both on the big, glass coffee table in front of me.

"Here! Figured you'd want something to drink, too."

"Thanks. Seriously, thank you so much. And I know this is going to sound weird, but can you, uh, just sit here until Mr. Oliver arrives? I'll pay you just the same."

He grinned, plopping down on the couch across from me as if he were excited to help.

"Sure! I'll tell you about my wife when she had our little girl. Maybe it'll take your mind off things."

As he spoke, I typed up a text to Jack.

It's happening. Come home now, call the doctor on the way here.

The response came moments later.

Holy shit. Got it. Be there in fifteen.

The contraction faded, and I smiled at the mover. "Please, do."

With that, he went into the story of the day his wife gave birth. He was a natural storyteller, getting me wrapped up in the epic tale of how his daughter, Lily, came into the world. I barely noticed the time pass.

It wasn't long before Jack showed up. Even in labor, it was impossible to ignore how handsome he was. He was dressed in professional clothes—gray slacks, black Oxfords, and a white button up with the top two buttons undone.

"There's my girl," he said, hurrying over and scooping me out of my seat. "You ready to have these twins?"

"Sure am, handsome." Just having him there with me was more than enough to calm me down.

We thanked Mick for his hard work and extra duties, making sure to leave him a huge tip for the day. Prepacked go-bag in hand, we were out the door.

Jack drove as carefully as he could in our new Land Rover while still hurrying us along as quickly as was reasonable. The contractions came faster and closer together, and by the time we arrived at the hospital I felt ready to pop.

The nurses did their thing, wheeling me into the delivery room, the space as bright and sunny and lovely as I could've hoped for. The gang slowly showed up—first Janie, then Mom and Dad, then Beau and Megan, who was already a few months pregnant herself.

Labor was intense and exhausting, but after nearly twelve hours of support and encouragement, we were rewarded with two gorgeous little fraternal twins, a boy and a girl.

Once the frenzy of the cleaning, weighing and checking fingers and toes was all done, Jack and I were alone with our babies for a few precious moments.

"Adam," he said, holding the boy, a perfect little man with the same dark hair and ice blue eyes as his father. "That's what we're going to call him."

"Allison," I said, cradling my little girl with my same light features.

It wouldn't be long before the rest of the gang came in to see the twins. For those few moments, however, there was nothing but peace and silence and love in that room.

So much damn love.

EPILOGUE II

JACK

Adam was barely a year-and-a-half-old, but I still couldn't get over how damn fast the kid got around.

"Easy, boy!" I said, feeling a breeze on my leg and looking up to see nothing but a flash of dark hair zooming by and leaving a wicked laugh in its wake. He hurried over to the other side of the living room, stopping when he was at the wall and turning to flash me the sort of mischievous smile that made it clear he was up to trouble.

I couldn't help but laugh myself, hurrying over to the little man and scooping him off the ground.

"Come 'ere, bud!"

Adam laughed like a madman as I flipped him over, pulled up his shirt to expose his chubby belly, and blew a raspberry against his skin. Nothing made me happier than the sound of my little guy laughing.

Well, aside from the sound of my little lady laughing.

When I'd had my fun with Adam, I set him down for some more roaming, keeping my eye on him all the while. I'd needed the distraction. After all, as soon as I'd put him down, the nervousness that had been running through me all day returned with a vengeance.

Buddy seemed to sense it, coming over and licking my hand. He was good with emotions like that. All the same, it was hard to wrap my head around the idea that I was nervous. I'd always taken pride in my calmness, my ability to stay unflappable in any situation.

Not that morning. I had more jitters running through me than I'd ever had before in my life. And there was only one woman to blame. I smiled as I stepped over to the window of the cabin, looking out over the back stretch of land, the two most important women in my life out there.

The backyard had gotten quite a makeover. The formerly open land was now surrounded with a tall, wooden fence that I'd built myself, a big play area for the twins off to the right. There was so much space back there, and every time I looked at it, I found myself dreaming of the future, picturing the playground I'd build when they were big enough, imagining playing catch with the kids when they'd grown old enough to toss a ball.

The future truly seemed boundless, full of hope and possibility. However, there was one thing I needed to do first before it could begin.

As if sensing my hesitation, Buddy whined next to me, licking my hand once more.

"I know, I know. I'm gonna do it, alright?" I cleared my throat and turned my attention back toward the yard.

Beth was out there with Ally, wearing a light-colored sundress and no shoes, laughing as she chased our little girl around the grass. The way the sun streamed down, catching them with beams of golden light that cut through the trees was like something out of a dream. I could watch them play all day like that; maybe joining in myself every now and then.

Adam plodded around out of the corner of my eye, approaching Buddy and once more enticing him to give chase. Buddy was happy to go along with it, letting out an excited bark as he fled from Adam as quickly as he could.

I placed my hand on my pocket, feeling the box inside and once more attempting to rally my nerves.

The last year and a half had been quite something for our little family. Adam and Ally were growing up so damn fast, turning more and more into little people with each passing day. Between motherhood and work, Beth kept herself quite busy. Wasn't easy being the mother of twins *and* the owner-operator of one of the fastest-growing wedding planning outfits in the city, but she stayed on top of it.

Just as I'd expected, once word—and pictures—of Beau and Megan's wedding got around, she had potential clients coming out the wazoo. She'd expanded her business to a staff of nearly a dozen, putting a few more killer weddings under her belt. I couldn't have been prouder of her and couldn't wait to see what new heights she'd reach over the next few years.

Beau and Megan hadn't been crazy about New York. After six months or so of living there, they'd found themselves yearning for the sights and smells and sounds of everything else in Colorado. Eventually, they cracked. Megan, wanting to raise my grandson—a gorgeous little boy named Theodore, where she'd grown up—quit her job, my son and his little family moving back to Colorado. That was more than fine with me. Being a grandpa was almost as much fun as being a new dad all over again.

I'd even had some new developments in my life, aside

from the little tykes, that is. Working freelance here and there had been fine, but the more I re-entered the wider world, the more I felt that itch to get out there and establish myself once again. To that end, I formed *Lynchpin Investments*, a small firm that handled the numbers of some of the highest earners in the city. I loved it. I set my own hours and made some damn good money in the process.

The last year had been something else. I couldn't wait for what the next had to offer.

Adam's laughter filled the air, blending with the sounds of Buddy's paws skittering on the wooden floor. When they started to get too wild, I opened the door and let them run outside, following them out and enjoying the sensation of the cool grass on my bare feet.

"Afternoon, handsome." Beth glanced up at me from where she was playing with Ally.

"Afternoon, gorgeous." I leaned in, kissing her softly on the lips, a kiss that, for a moment, turned into something a little more heated.

"That was... unexpected," she said with a smile.

"Hard to contain myself with you sometimes, darlin'."

She smiled in a manner that made it obvious it was more than appreciated. I leaned over and planted another little kiss on Ally's chubby cheek. She smiled at me in response, waving her hand before turning her attention back to her toys.

"Well, believe it or not," Beth said, "I think these two are ready for a nap."

"Yeah, I just spotted Adam yawning over there."

"Want to help me get them down? I'm thinking they're both due for a bath, but that can wait until tonight."

"Sounds perfect."

Together, we gathered up the kids and started our pre-nap routine. I loved it. Few things were more nourishing to the soul than the routines with our little ones, getting them changed and fed and put down, reading them a story or two and watching their eyelids grow heavier by the moment.

Pretty soon they were asleep, their little chests rising and falling gently. I kissed them both on the forehead, Beth and I leaving the room soon after and shutting the door quietly behind us. The second it was closed, I knew there was no more putting it off. I turned to Beth and spoke.

"I need to—"

"—talk to you about something."

We finished our sentences at the same time, breaking out into nervous smiles.

"Looks like we've both got some matters on our minds," I said.

"Sounds like it."

"Why don't we go out onto the balcony and talk it over."

She nodded, her lips pursed together in a tight, nervous sort of way. What on earth did she have to tell me, and why did it make her so nervous?

Together we headed out onto the balcony, another new addition to the cabin that I'd built myself. The view was gorgeous, the valley lush and green, the sky a perfect, clear blue. Once we were seated next to one another, we both took deep breaths in preparation for whatever was to come.

"Well," I said. "Looks like we need to figure out who goes first."

She quickly nodded. "Yeah. I've got something to tell you or, rather, to *show* you."

I placed my hand on my pocket, outlining the box with my fingertip.

"Same here, actually."

"So... why don't we just, you know, take 'em out at the same time?"

"Alright. On three?"

"On three."

"One."

"Two."

"*Three!*"

In my hand was a diamond ring, the stone big and gorgeous enough to shimmer in the sun. She gasped, her eyes going wide. When I saw what was in *her* hand, my eyes did a little widening of their own.

It was a pregnancy test.

"Is that...?" I asked.

She nodded. "It sure is. And does that mean...?" She nodded toward the ring.

"It sure does."

Beth held fast for a moment, then let out a squeal of delight. "Yes!" She shouted. "I will!"

My heart bursting with joy, I slipped the ring onto her finger, wrapped my arm around her, and took the test into my hand.

"You ready for this?" I asked.

Beth grinned. "Ready."

"I love you, gorgeous."

"I love you too, handsome."

The future had somehow grown even brighter. I couldn't wait to dive right into it.

THE END

Printed in Dunstable, United Kingdom